JOANA AGAINST MY WILL

Marcelo Mirisola

JOANA AGAINST MY WILL

1st Edition
POD

Petrópolis
KBR
2012

Text edition **Noga Sklar**
Translation **Fal Azevedo**
Cover **Caco Galhardo**

ISBN: 978-85-8180-153-7

KBR Editora Digital Ltda.
www.kbrdigital.com.br
atendimento@kbrdigital.com.br
55|24|2222.3491

B869 - Brazilian Literature

Obra publicada com o apoio do
Ministério da Cultura do Brasil/Fundação Biblioteca
Nacional / Centro Internacional do Livro
**Published with the support of
Ministério da Cultura do Brasil/Fundação Biblioteca Na-
cional / Centro Internacional do Livro**

Printed in Brazil

 **Marcelo Mirisola** is considered one of the biggest re-
velations in the Brazilian Literature of the 1990s. He
graduated from Law School, but never became a law-
yer. He is known for his innovative and daring style,
and the sometimes virulent way he reacts against the
status quo and the "fraternities" of the literary world.
He has also written *Funk, The Returned Hero, Bungalow* and *The Blue
Of The Deceased Son. Joana Against My Will* is his first novel transla-
ted to English.

Email: marcelomirisola@yahoo.com.br

To my missing daughter.

An acknowledgement

*To Patricia Cornils,
with whom I shared a nightmare.*

There it is: We are slaves of the female's desire, or we are nothing. As my old man used to say: "If you feel deaf to the clamor of the beautiful sex, you would better close yourself in the cloisters. All of them are bitches"... And I, who by then was around 11 years old, added: "Thank God!"

José Carlos Oliveira

Table of Contents

JOANA AGAINST MY WILL

I fucked Joana five times without a condom, which made me feel proud and flattered—at first, more because of the quantity than of any emotional closeness. If only I hadn't made the stupid mistake of wanting to love her at the same time.

This kind of situation that happened three weeks ago, before I got the first email, was inconceivable and totally unlike me. "There goes my ass," I thought.

I don't know if I'm still the same lonely guy now as I was before, fiercely against the mammalian instincts of human beings. After all that has happened, I don't know. My friend Reinaldo Moraes once told me: "One day, you'll come inside the woman who loves you." Maybe some variation of that prophecy had come true. Or had I come inside a hole that loved me?

Is Joana the hole where I've now buried myself? Is that all?

I don't know, I don't know. Maybe I'm just "being melodramatic". Well, there are two things of which I am certain: I left my sperm inside of her, together with all these doubts, and, for one night, Joana freed me from the sentimental misery of the past forty years. Oh God.

The next morning, she refused to answer my call. She told me to call her some other day.

I understood something else. Besides freeing me from the sentimental misery of forty years, she had killed our child with the morning-after pill. She was sleepy. For the first time, someone other than me and my loneliness managed to kill something that had been half-created inside of me. It wasn't fiction. I decided to insist. She deserved it. So did I. Sooner or later, Joana would answer. Of course she would, and when she did, for the first time in those domestic circumstances, I would love a woman as though I was really fucking her.

I knew it wouldn't be easy for Joana to get rid of the half of me that was inside her. I could bet. I had Viagra on my side and a whole procession of dead souls in the graveyards (most call them books; it makes no difference to me) that I had published and that she so admired. It was such foolishness. If Joana would only answer my calls or incorporate the fictional demon with open legs, saying, "That's the way you wanted it, so eat me out now." That was exactly the way I wanted it.

Without a doubt, Joana was the best missionary position experience of my life. She had the softest, roundest ass I'd ever known, and a tongue that always worked in circular, spiraling motions. Those motions were great for both a tentative kiss (I'll talk more about the kiss later) and for oral sex. The latter was surprisingly better than the missionary position. While I can't say we understood each other, it would be unfair to Joana's tongue and the small flaw in her teeth to say that we didn't. The blow job had other advantages—an à la carte pussy, and Joana all around it.

So, we fucked. And it was amazing. And she didn't come, and told me the problem was hers. I was head over heels.

Joana was waxed, the old-fashioned way. "Just for you, my love," she said. "Just for me!"

Oh my God, the kiss. Joana entered that motel room

like a blind woman, beautiful and hesitant. She licked me diagonally trying to find, something that wasn't there. She surrounded me with a kiss that didn't exist (one that I am still trying to understand). The kiss both pulled me closer to and pushed her away from that uncertain place—that "licked spot." I was swept away and I wanted to know if Joana was "real" and she answered me with her straight hair, not even trying to distinguish "truth" from "lie" since she was my invention, my unfolding that kept running away from me. I couldn't even reach her tongue. But the pull was too strong and we took our excitement and our misunderstandings to bed. She wouldn't look me in the eyes not because she was blind. I understand now it was because I was responsible for the kiss that never was, and Joana, as we had previously arranged, was drunk on whiskey. "I'll be waiting for you at midnight, my love, at the motel, drunk on whiskey, my love." I had to take her undoings and mine (never ours together) to the limit, and that meant I had to tear off her black panties and shove my dick inside of her and try, even though I knew something was wrong about it, to kiss her and fuck her at the same time. I had to forget my machinations and focus only on the sperm that I would pour inside of her. I could make some sort of exchange, killing the fiction and taking "the real woman" in my arms. But if we had anything in common, it was only vertigo, and the vertigo, despite being equivalent, wasn't a collusion. There was actually some imbalance as she tried to dodge my movements, either pretending or trying to believe in herself. I kept thrusting, still thinking I had "the real woman" in my arms.

The situation didn't allow for retreating. So, I can't understand after all that had happened, how she could turn away, or how she didn't suffer from the same loneliness that I did. If she was simultaneously the repository of all of my love and the fruit of all my curses and prayers, then how could she have walked away? Hadn't I invented her? Yes, me, with my own spunk, believing for the first time in my life that I had gotten rid of all my sarcasm and indifference and that "sperm" and "spunk" were the same thing I mean I wasn't there, in that second-class motel room to write another book. I was there to get her pregnant and dodge the death inside of her (even my selfish self said yes), as if reality could challenge the giant and be greater than my internal fire, divided only between us, two chimpanzees, Joana and me, a reality separated from talent and larger than damnation. Why not?

Could Joana have been aware of both the disgrace and the greatness that our fucking might produce? I suspect that perhaps she preferred to ignore what I decided to call "the curse that contains the whole miracle." Or perhaps it wasn't her time. Perhaps she'd had some kind of distorted perception, running away from the kiss, as if she could sense the abyss, seeking some defense from herself and my creation. It made no difference. Everything was a spiraling mix of excitement, hesitant kisses and Rio de Janeiro, and Joana had nothing to do with any of it! After all, I was the one who involved her in that story and climaxed, completely alone, in the most pathetic, predictable way inside of her womb. What had she done? Well, I believed that she did what had to be done. No more and no less than excluding me and the little Indian, my daughter, that she killed with the morning-after pill. If I were Joana, I'd have done the same, even if by instinct alone.

So, we tacitly shared creation, abortion and a love that wouldn't survive the attraction or the morning after; it would die even before the flesh became rotten or fecund. It was all the same. The guilt and the spunk, however, were all mine. I didn't want to scorn Joana because she took care of it herself. She's a lunatic, a daughter of the abyss, inevitable as the morning after death. No, I won't do that (for now, Hell is all mine). Shit! I was the one who created her. I was the one who had given her the abyss. It had all been my fault. I filled Joana with my sperm to save myself (myself, my God! Not her) from the curse of flying over the abyss, of being the non-tongue, of running away without leaving a phone number or an address. How could she have acted like that?

I would do things my way then.

I shouldn't have been surprised. She followed the proper itinerary that I had ultimately established for myself, the love itinerary, whose last strike is annihilation. It is simply the itinerary that kills some and invents others. The curse lies in a place of perpetual loneliness, the "forever ever after." Only for one night, Joana went through all of the steps. She both killed and died, although she couldn't even suspect nor could have the slightest perception of this when she ran so rightfully from that kiss. The fugitive kiss. That's how the kiss was.

As for fucking, I can say we were in the same condition. At least in the same physical condition, of that I have no doubt. But Joana was taking a greater risk. She could get many diseases and eventually conceive a child, but she still opened herself to me, placing all of her bets on me (on me?). The difference was that I was fucking myself and placing all my bets on us and I believed that Joana was doing the same.

I took my woman as if I had the responsibility of the Holy Ghost to impregnate the Virgin Mary, although I couldn't care less about the long-term result. To me, it didn't matter if the fruit of our passion was Jesus Christ or a retard; what mattered was that we were having "an honest fuck," (at least on my part I can guarantee that) and by fucking that way we could continue on with our lives. There wasn't really another way of fucking; even mice fuck the same way, and they would never know the happiness of escaping from a kiss. We, on the other hand (I believed), knew we weren't mice and that was why we didn't feel the need for "protection," wearing a condom, or taking pills, or checking the calendar. We just had to run away from each other. How could two condemned people protect themselves from "forever?" I had no more and no less than "the curse that contains the whole miracle" or "forever" in my arms. So, it was an honest fuck. My first. Joana behaved like an elliptical lizard. As I thrust more and more violently, I could sense her feet kicking the air, trying desperately to find anchorage on my ribs. That excited me even more, and I tried to reach her stomach with my dick, and moved my body forward with the intention of suffocating her with my shoulders (See what the missionary position can make you do?). If she lost her breath, I imagined she would die in my arms and go straight to heaven at that moment. Joana was focused on making circular movements with her tongue inside my mouth, which confused and excited me and made me pull back and go easy on the thrusts so she could breathe again and kick her feet in the air. I think she did that in self-defense.

Those circular kisses and that spiraling movement that Joana used to lick the base of my shaft have a name, something that resembles a hat. Or something with a brim and a crown that could receive those spiraling licks. It should be said that this "something" was much more than just a blow job. It was both exciting and comforting because it let me fall on my back, resting, after all that thrusting. I don't know if "rest" and "comfort" are the right words, but I know that Joana was working for me and that was only the beginning.

I came to understand her kiss and I knew her teeth. It was as if Joana opened up little by little, or as if she had a vagina in her mouth. With all the nuances, her upper and bottom lips, and the reverberations down there, she had the advantage of a thick tongue that kissed me in spirals (the same way that she sucked my dick). My arms were shaking and I lost my balance a few times, slipping. So I was knocked out and she rode me again. Another specialty of Joana's was that she seemed to become a tongue, licking my body as an invertebrate animal, as though she had the ability to fold herself over, inventing another body for me (like hers). It was as though she could lie on my dick without bending it. We moved backward and forward without really moving, until the moment we separated.

"I didn't come." That was what she told me, lighting a cigarette.

I opened a can of beer, and offered a sip to Joana, who reciprocated with an icy kiss. Very good. The conversation stalled, and I tried to change the tone, or find a way of fixing, through my words, Joana's "mammalian lapse."

"You didn't?" I asked. "That's your problem."

She agreed and laughed. She was the fan, a bedroom mirror, she was myself, something that could fool me and fool itself because of a good story we had invented, a story that, thinking it over, we had taken to an end. Together. Actually (I discovered two days later), Joana knew the fact that our fuck hadn't been as good as my comment, "That's your problem," and that fact would only make the comment true. I mean, you can't fuck only with words, although sometimes this is wiser and necessary. It was curious. On all fours that round ass wasn't that attractive. It was only enchanting. I think I should have slapped that white butt. The problem is I would certainly go about it with too much intensity. I'd never slapped a woman. It's better not to hit, I thought, than to hit too strongly.

But when Joana was on her side, she knew how to ask for a dick, and in that moment I experienced another first. That is, I invested "my dick" in her and occasionally my dick was behind Joana's ass (That ass would accept anything. It could have been a Pataxo Indian or a toucan's beak, whatever). From that point on, I could hold her by her thighs as I'd never done with a woman before. My entire flesh was against her flesh, which always moved in spirals and in the opposite direction. For me, it was the best of all four fucks. Before that, I had sucked her tits, by demand, "Suck, suck my tits," then went into the second phase of that spiraling kiss.

The best moment for Joana, she confessed later, was between the third and the fourth time, when I whispered in her ear, "Open your legs." Well, I don't know now if she "confessed" that or if I had the impression that she did. Despite all of the acrobatics, Joana was my "woman" and she obeyed me. "Open, open your little legs."

In the end, just as we were bridging fiction with reality, the receptionist called, telling us our time was over. I left with a hard-on. I had come five times inside Joana. No, we didn't really fit.

AN OLD CARIOCA NIGHT

If I said we had been sucked in by or that we had jumped into an old carioca night, I would be using a cliché. However, I think that after such a classic fuck, and in such circumstances, Joana and I deserved all the clichés that could swallow us, drag us, suck us into the night. The lightness, in any case, was less of an obligatory presence and more of a partner of our shadows and the almost empty Largo do Machado. The streets were evidently filthy, and a beggar took a dump on the pavement in front of Hotel Serrano. There was nothing magical about that place, but the night was really old, I swear it was. So, I was a little ashamed to hold Joana's hand. I don't know, maybe I thought it would slip from mine. I didn't know what to do. Maybe I didn't have the vocation to "lead her" or to look into her eyes etc., and we weren't a good match anyway. She was more interested in answering her mobile and talking to her friend than being "led" through a sad, ancient night by a sadder, embarrassed guy who, besides trying to conceal a hard-on, was scared shitless of being killed on the next corner. Joana walked quickly and, while she laughed on the phone, told me to relax because she was used to the carioca nights and had "three Arab entities" protecting her. I believed her, proud of the Arab entities that protected her, and definitely felt drawn to her, and distant. At that moment, I had one of my worst and most beautiful moments of solitude—I was not participating in all of that, and didn't have the option of being included. It was a mix of tenderness and wreckage; this was my feeling for that girl who dragged me around, in spite of the old night, in spite of myself.

If things weren't fitting, or if we had an ancient (and sad) end to the night ahead of us, at least we were in the company of our shadows and doubts, worst case scenario. That was beautiful. It felt like we knew each other too well, before time and beyond sex, and regardless of the giggles she exchanged with the friend on the phone. "It was awesome, I'll call you later." I laughed and agreed with everything, until the moment I managed to hold Joana's hand. She immediately tried to get rid of me, saying that she had to find something in her bag, maybe a pill.

We crossed the square where José de Alencar used to sit and wait for eternity, my Iracema and I[1], before the wordplay that was genius. In five minutes, turning to the right, we would arrive at Café Lamas, a narrow bar with a checkered floor. That's what I remember. I also remember old-fashioned waiters, cracked mirrors and the little vampires.

Joana's friends. A chubby girl dressed like Friday the 13th, totally out of time and place (this disturbed me; everyone was out of time and place) didn't answer Joana's greeting, downright ignoring her. That rejection humanized the gesture made by "my girlfriend" and brought her closer to me, to my lack of grace. Ah, that was the first thing (apart from sex) that we had in common. I celebrated to myself and made no comment. A girl came to hug her. It made no difference to me. I

---

1 Editors' note: Jose Alencar was a 19th century Brazilian author who wrote *Iracema* about the relationship between an indigenous woman and a Portuguese colonist.

ordered a beer and stayed there, anesthetized.

It didn't make any difference because, before experiencing jealousy, I had to enjoy the company of my first girlfriend. That was it. It was my social debut as a "taken" man after forty years, as if I had jumped from the agricultural phase of romance to the robotics of sexual excitement, without having listened to the Brasilia rock bands of my adolescence, a period when I had wisely locked myself in the maid's tiny room.

I greeted people around me, known and unknown to Joana—"How are you?," "Good evening," "What's up?," and made an effort to leave her at ease, "my girlfriend." My first one. Joana watched my efforts twice, and then called me closer. She gave me little wet kisses. I don't know, maybe I was just showing off to the little vampires who couldn't care less about her. If I wanted to survive that bar after the best fuck of my life with a girl twenty years younger, I would have to act like an uncle. And that was what I did. After all, it couldn't have been different. I think I was a jerk, but a jerk in the right measure—to keep due distance or to separate things that, without noticing, I had mixed and lost forever. I ordered another beer. She didn't follow me, and I wanted to play the badass. I ordered another, and told her that after five fucks, I had to drink at least ten beers. The problem was that I regretted the joke immediately. Instead of looking into Joana's eyes as she looked into mine, I extended the joke and "discussed" various subjects. The result was that we definitively lost the spiralling desire that a few hours earlier had brought us together under the sheets. Until the moment Joana felt defeated and seemed to wilt. But she still looked beautiful.

Morning came. We were the last ones to leave Lamas, and our fuck seemed to be more and more distant. On the sidewalk, we hugged for a long time. That was the first reconciliation, I believe. Or better, now I understand. I woke a taxi driver and helped Joana get into the car. Before the taxi left, she called me from the window and gave me another little kiss. For a fleeting moment, I was certain that the hug and the little kiss were better than the five fucks. If not better, at least more human, more beautiful, and that beauty would eventually bring her back. From where, exactly, I wasn't sure. After all, I could never imagine that Joana would leave forever, and that it would be the first and last time she would be with me.

Our different paths in life brought us closer to something definite, something cheesy, that is, we had somehow "built a past together," regardless of the farewell and the next day. She waved from the taxi with a sad look on her face.

The last kiss. The first, too. The long hug that followed—the most beautiful, cinematographic and passionate one that I ever got. The old night had finished with all of my expectations. Two days later, she would tell me she had wanted to puke, and that it had been the most beautiful night in her life. She was happy.

I WANT TO TRY TO UNDERSTAND WHY I GOT HERE

In spite of all the hully-bully, and after five genius books, I'm still a lonely, dislocated person, pathetically furious and always with the feeling that I've never moved an inch forward. I haven't achieved anything in life. Or worse, I've corrupted and destroyed everything I loved and hated.

Joana stayed with me until the end. I don't know if she was the "real woman," or the "only woman I have met in all my life," or the woman responsible for the fact that I reached this point, defeated and totally sceptical about my future, about love and all its sub-products and unfoldings. I honestly don't know.

She was a bitch to me. Maybe I wasn't such a jerk to her, maybe we have set the record straight.

We trampled over each other. It must have been love. It was crap.

On my part, before her, way before her, I had thought that being honest to myself and "playing the badass" indiscriminately would help me get rid of myself, be happy and have the rest I that deserved. Idiot, I was an idiot. I just blew myself up, and took Joana with me (although she helped with the process). The fact is that I lost the enchantment of my first suicidal days; even those I shared with Joana. Before her, I chose sacrifice, and was reborn, stronger and stronger every time. Now, that didn't happen.

If I just said that it was difficult to get where we were, and that after everything I didn't know what to do at the airport, and that the money I earned writing about my nothingness and the nothingness of others only made me walk in circles like a dizzy cockroach, and that if I depended on her, I would never know where to go, and that she had been my guide and without her I would have never arrived at this nonplace. And if I said that I made sure to not wear a condom because I believed in Joana and believed that all my ailing would end inside of her, or even if I said again that by leaving me she gave me back to myself (which is way more serious), or if I said that the only thing that made me happy, after Joana, was a little heart-of-palm pastry that I ate at the Santos Dumont airport, and if I repeated everything my memory and the lack of it tell me to save myself from Joana (among other things), I wouldn't have gotten here, stumbling and still a little lucid after all.

If I repeated the same flight, looking at Rio de Janeiro from above, I would only be singing a sad version of "Samba do Avião," the farewell version. Yet, I would take with me only the books I wrote. If Rio wasn't so gray outside, and if the Christ's head hadn't been hidden by clouds of Bismuth Magnesia, I wouldn't be able to talk about Joana. Unfortunately, that's how it is. This is what interests me, and I don't want to miss a thing.

Above all, I don't want to leave her out of the damage we caused each other. I confess it would be too easy if I said I fell in love again with the wrong woman. The problem is that she made the same stupid mistake and fell in love with the wrong man, isn't it? I don't know. Oh God! Why couldn't I do it? It was Joana who did what I should have done, wasn't it? She was the asshole. She made the pacts and committed murder in my place, didn't she? No, I can't accept this idea.

First of all, I can't accept this because I started writing with fire. Something burned in my esophagus and I had to say no. Then, I wanted the world. Not this stupid little world I had achieved and that attracted Joana so strongly; I wanted the *zeitgeist* all for myself and ended up roaming the bars of Vila Madalena, making a fool of myself and drinking myself into a stupor with a bunch of second-rate writers who could only stab me in the back. Stupid, talentless people. Joana could take me somewhere else, and only her. If it weren't for Joana, I would end up minimally successful. And on the day I wanted to rekindle the fire that consumed me before everything happened, they would tell me (as they did) to shut my mouth, because they were my friends and cared about me. Ah, Joana.

I can't say I was betrayed. I can't say I betrayed, either. What happened was Joana led me on because I had nowhere to go. It is simple—I didn't exchange the nothingness of life in Vila Madalena for the life of the beggar who crossed the street because I didn't have the guts to do so (and I would probably have regretted it, but that's another story), and everything I had, to make a long story short, was reaching almost the same level of those little writers of the Vila. Would Joana save me if I wasn't like them?

No, it's not that. Joana was better.

To a certain extent, I have to be grateful to Joana. In spite of everything, here I am, repeating the same mistake of writing another book to get rid of myself and ultimately to get rid of her, Joana.

This was the exchange I made, although I didn't want to, which means something.

But I have to admit that the kick in the ass was didactic. Yes, I'll admit it. Oh my God.

It isn't worth it to go into such details, as the sun rising in Copacabana's Posto Três[2] after our chimpanzee night, and Joana waving at me from the taxi, looking sad. What matters is that most of the time Joana gave me the ammunition to commit the murder I chose (which actually chose us, by the way). Yet, we arranged our first and last meeting. We made a bet on each other. Until the end. "If we want to crash, let's crash at full speed." Well, that had been our agreement since the first e-mail we had exchanged.

It didn't matter that that thing (our meeting?) was unavoidable. At first, the freedom of the flight was the only condition to fly. Is it cheesy? Of course it is. But we made our bet. I was even more of a fool, a total hillbilly, and I made a bet in love. She doubled the offer and added sex to the lost game. What a woman. A slut. Beautiful. Enchanted.

Having a woman like Joana is not something easy that can be solved with a good fuck. She gave me what I needed to face the worst of my enemies, which was and still is loneliness. I was lucky, because I understood I had become a jerk. I owe this to Joana. With no exaggeration. A true love exists for this, to look after you and ease your worst moments of solitude. The rest are just appearances; sex, the piston moving in and out. A chimpanzee arena.

Cheers to solitude then.

What monster is this? The first thing to do as one responds to the monster is to know who asks in its name. If it is the guy who three weeks ago still believed (ah, what insistence) in a love affair with a view of the ocean, the answer would evidently be grief, death, pain and agony, and absolute failure in all aspects. Now, if the question is answered by the guy who is writing, the answer is that it's all of this and a little death, failure, pain and agony with a beautiful view of the

---

2 Editors' note: Posto Três is the third of six "Postos" into which Copacabana Beach is divided.

wavy ocean in Leme beach. One way or another, the most important thing is to know that regardless of the occasion and in spite of who this monster is and who he asks for, the answer is the same. Joana didn't want me. End of story.

VILA MADALENA, SIX MONTHS AGO

At that time, I was looking for a true woman (it sounds like a joke). I had just met Marcia Denser and read her book *Diana the Hunter*. Marcia survived herself, differently from Ana C. and Sylvia Plath. Those are four women (now I include Joana) that haunt me and that, let's say, "did what had to be done." Marcia and Joana are alive, are flesh and blood beings. Marcia is a ghost of herself and Joana is my ghost. I'm reaching, I know, when I make this comparison, but I have to bring them closer to get somewhere. As for the fact that Marcia didn't kill herself, I would say that this option—despite Marcia's living ghost and her redundant survival—is proof that the supernatural works against the supernatural. That is, she, Marcia Denser, became an incubus of her own work, the most vehement and clear form of condemnation and confrontation a writer could ever offer herself and her writers. She reached a glory half posthumous, half pepperoni, in the saddest, most sublime way.

I don't know if Joana could carry such weight. Honestly, as a man in love, this is the last thing I'd wish for her. Or else I wanted Joana to breed a hatch, and never really became interested in her fortuitous "literary skills." I was sick of the eternal, do you understand? Nevertheless, it was as a writer that she came to me. She was interested in herself, and she needed an alibi or an "equal" who would say yes. I said yes. Of course I did. Joana would wait for me, already drunk on whiskey.

Let me speak a little more about Marcia Denser. I visited her the other day, because she had just had her uterus removed (I'm not really sure, with Marcia it could have been a Kent mango core. Whatever). The removal of the "thing" had happened recently. Marcia gave me a warm welcome, looking excited and less swollen than I had supposed. We listened to ghost tangos on a ghost vitrola, we fed each other's foolish vampirisms, and she drank two bottles of sweet wine alone. It was around two in the afternoon, I think. She gave me a few pills and prescribed me some antacids that "take shit out of you like a hand." The telephone rang.

"Hello. I know, I know. I'll tell you what you do—take some Prozac. I'm busy now, M.M. is here. Bye."

Ah, Marcia. What a professional. That was typical of a generous vampire, a Piazzolla fan. Then she showed me the love letters that Lobo Antunes had written to her in the eighties, and I was a bit relieved to know that Marcia had been his Joana, and that the author of *Judas's Asses* had managed to be much cheesier, more delusional and sappy than I'm being right now, although he hadn't made the affair public. But that's alright.

I won't reveal the sugary details of the correspondence, because I honestly admire Lobo Antunes and made some abhorrent calculations after reading his letters. Well, if the Portuguese man who deserved a Nobel Prize in Saramago's place had written those banalities because of a lost love, then my kicked ass and I deserved at least two Nobels, for Peace and for Literature. The first one for having felt as stupid as Lobo Antunes and, in spite of that, having spared Marcia (Joana's mirror) when she cried for the lost love of the *Portuga* she herself had killed, and the second because my prose was infinitely better than Lobo Antunes's and Saramago's combined. So, according to my calculations, the Nobel Foundation owed me two million dollars, maybe three. And then they would have to invent a new category for not having understood what those two cruel, hollow pussies (one without a womb and a soul, the other without me) wanted and did to me—The Nobel Prize for Haunting.

This meant that Marcia was the real woman, now more than ever. A prelude to Joana (?), emptied of her primordial poison, the womb. Unfortunately, I have to recognize that Joana is a serious candidate to get there. Maybe she will end up mad, drunk, hollow and funny like Marcia, maybe she will take the same path as Ana C., Sylvia Plath and her own mother...and kill herself. Who knows? What I know is that these women haunt me, and before Joana arrived, the clingiest one was Ana C. That one was truly an evil spirit, a curse, and I only got rid of her when I found Reinaldo Moraes. He humanized the "thing" and himself. I admire him for being the author of *Whatever* and especially for having been able to escape his own greatness. This is humanity. I envy him. I'd really like to have the ability that he had to assimilate this shitty life as it shouldn't be. A big hug, my friend.

But I was in Vila Madalena. And I was talking about an "against the counter" situation. When I was looking for the "real woman," I wandered around posh bars such as the Canto Madalena. I liked to call that place a "deliberately casual" bar. Let me explain. A guy eats nostalgic yellow eggs and tidbits typical of the fifties. The furniture and the decoration are convincing, and as a true *habitué*, he actually believes that João Gilberto and the Bossa Nova gang exist and, worst of all, invents women who don't exist to help him with this carefully calculated jingoism, meaning he feels very at ease. The problem is, when it's time to pay the bill he gets royally fucked. A beer costs four reais, the waiters are troglodytes and the environment is perfect for the parade of Guevara berets, colorful suspenders, an incredible lack of talent and the official release of generational anthologies. Sometimes, we fall into the trap and end up paying other people's bills. And then, Suzi Chang enters the picture.

She was a friend of a friend of someone who shares an apartment with two nice girls who are dating (yes, both of them) a cousin of a friend of someone who, surprisingly, isn't gay! Actually, Suzi wasn't a Jap, but a Korean, and wouldn't deny her origin, although she was used to telling the same story over and over—she wasn't a Jap, but a Korean, and that meant that besides being someone's friend and sharing the apartment with somebody's cousin who wasn't gay, she had a "fantasy." Ah, a fantasy!

When I heard the Jap talking about fantasies, I woke up from my stupor immediately. I remembered my dear Wanderlei. Even the Wanderlei whose name is spelled not with a "W" but with a "V" has fantasies.

"Even Vanderlei!" I said.

The comment was ignored. I didn't care. I had already registered Vanderlei's "fantasies" in my *Returned Hero* and Suzi, the Jap, I mean, the Korean, lit her cigarette off of another and talked cheerfully about her bipolarities and fantasies. She wanted to be "a street whore, a really cheap one, the kind that has an apartment in a cheap hotel."

She worked in a law office and used to go to *ofuro* houses. A total bitch. So I took ten reais from my pocket and told her, "Right away, little Jap girl. I'm going to make your fantasy come true, but you'll have to do what I want." Suzi Chang retreated. Suzi, who wasn't a Jap, but a Korean, told me she was Korean and closed the subject by saying I was a jerk. It was always like that. I was the jerk who ruined other people's fantasies. By the way, there are some assholes, artist-wannabes in the outskirts who always complain that I ruin their fantasies and threaten to kill me. Honestly, I couldn't care less about them. And I couldn't care less about the Suzi Changs of this life. They have fantasies. They are all the same, half-animals. That was why Marcia and Joana's charms hit me right on target. They are two real women. Women who faced me and, what was worse, haunted me until I lost my ten *reaus* and all understanding.

I have to open another parenthesis here. At that time, before I met Joana, I used to write (do I still write?) weekly chronicles on the internet that were way above average, and I used to be (am I still?) very well paid. So, I paid the bitches well. I almost always ruined the fantasies of the average internet surfer, and I had a lot of fun with that. I was even accused of being an "opinionator." Me! In spite of all the recriminations, I never took anything seriously. What is the problem with calling the President of the Republic a drunk and Father Marcelo a faggot? Isn't the first a politician and the second a saint? So, the first should just ignore me, and the second just forgive me. What I want to say is this—everything was perfectly under control, upside down, before I met Joana. I was a fucked-up guy, and it didn't matter if I was badly or well paid. Now, I don't know.

I lost control, and now Joana never leaves my thoughts. Before her, I didn't worry about understanding things and giving explanations. I was indifferent to Nelson Gonçalves singing "Lupicínio Rodrigues." I didn't cry so often. My motto was "fuck it." My epitaph was "fuck." Now, things have changed. Lately, I have had no other alternative but to be what I have never been. Look at that. If the Suzi Changs couldn't understand a joke (it didn't matter if it was a bad one) the greatest loss was ultimately mine, and I had never been able to share my talent with someone who really deserved it.

Joana was the only one who managed it. But before

talking about this, I would like to say that I felt truly happy to mess with the Suzi Changs of this life. I admit that my victims weren't ready for my well-designed cynicism and the tone of debauchery and sarcasm I used with such skill, almost surgically. Maybe they didn't deserve it. It was cowardice on my part and I recognize it. But that was my style, and I can't say I suffered because of it. Now it's different. Crap! Now it's different. I walked away from myself. I let my guard down. Oh my God. Before Joana, I used to believe in impeccable, rhetorical pieces. I knew that I could take a (deserved) fall at any moment, and I knew I could answer back with even more violence and brilliance. But Joana, I say it again and again, she was my end. I got lost.

The Beauty uses my own weapons, and I can't defend myself against my own poison. I see that my self-destructive blah blah blah was bullshit in face of the imposing immobility, in face of the love I feel for Joana. That was only an expedient I used to not give up, to attack first and leave unharmed. It was easy, to make a long story short, to adopt that attitude when I didn't really know what came after the iceberg.

When I told my desires to go fuck themselves, when I didn't depend on anyone, when I changed my star sign as I needed, when I had a few conveniences and a series of statements and variables which I manipulated regardless of everyone and everything and regardless of myself, and I still had time to identify the "right measure of the twisted arm" (meaning that when I didn't give myself away completely to the Paraguayan and let my guard down knowing that it was only a disguise, and thus, fucking it all up, came back from the dead without having died), *cazzo*! I can't say I was a happy guy. But I could count on myself and make miracles!

Why did Joana come into my life? She said we'd have children, go shopping together. She was going to be my little wife and I would protect her on her saddest days. She made me believe in rainy days.

Well, let me talk about a coincidence here. A week before Joana kicked my ass, I had read Primo Levi's *If This Is a Man,* taking into consideration the gravity and proportion of things. I believe Levi survived the concentration camp mainly because he could understand what I've decided to call "the right measure of the twisted arm." The question is, why, after having escaped the horror of Birkenau and written that stupendous book, did Levi kill himself in his old age?

The answer isn't that simple. Resisting life, I think, is an almost instinctive "choice." And, if a paradox like this can be exercised regardless of a more accurate reflection, the fact that one can renew it and live one day after the other is the same as half-thinking and half-existing (or almost instinctively). That is complete madness. Even knowing that you are no more than a dog biting your own tail, you still insist and demand too much of a Chimera, an "almost option." That is where this paradox crap comes from, and, in my case, it happened after watching the sunrise at Posto Três, after the chimpanzee night and after Joana waved goodbye from the taxi window. There is not, as I understood because of Joana, a point of balance or a point of unbalance that sustains human beings. It doesn't matter if they're in or out of love. What I can't understand is how most people can stand it until the end, and, at the same time, resist their own lack of verisimilitude.

This is what I imagined I had in common with Levi, in spite of all the woes and aggravations and before meeting Joana—the lack of verisimilitude. Well, I resisted the lack of verisimilitude! But that was before Joana.

I don't know what would become of me in a concentration camp. But if there was anything left, I would write a book. That I don't doubt at all. I would do it out of an implicit debt—to survive this so-called lack of verisimilitude.

And to hell with the paradoxes. Primo Levi resisted

the hardship as much as he could.

This was different from my affair with Joana. That girl fucked with my lack of verisimilitude, with my "almost option," with my instincts, with my reason, with my paradoxes, with my cojones and everything fucking else. It isn't easy to recognize the relevance she had, still has and will have in my life story. The only thing I know is that I write this book in spite of myself. She didn't have a crush on me. This is the crime Joana accuses me of, after five fucks, after the most beautiful night of my chimpanzee life.

Okay, no one is forced to have a crush on anyone, or to demand anything in return.

So here I am

And if Joana set the trap, it was only to become my character. I want to say she was successful. I'm writing another book for her, because of her and because, after all, we created a fiction together, not a lie. And it was this damned fiction that fucked me and promised a life of small things—fish dinners, a shared rent, children, pets, going to Serzedelo Correia street market, holding hands forever. Nothing could be more appropriate (in the name of this damned attraction that killed love) than inventing another name for her, or better, instead of a dedication, a death statement from the epigraph. Maybe this is the only answer to the perfect meeting, to the "forever" that Joana promised me and that I had (do I still have?) the means to return. With what? With the goddamn literature? That was what she wanted, an imitation of life, or that old story of sacrificing this shitty life for the sake of art. Was that all?

No, I don't think so. A great fuck and a gross mismatch?

What did Joana want? To spend a night with her favorite writer? "Fuck me, you're the best writer in Brazil?" So, she wanted the disease, the dementia and the fucked-up mind of the man who wrote my books? And instead of returning the feeling with what I didn't possess, I gave her my love, and it wasn't enough?

What should I have done? Should I have spanked her? Should I have left without paying the bill of that cheap hotel? Should I have been a jerk? Was that what she wanted?

Or maybe the problem wasn't me. Maybe she had included me in her little madness as if I had been an additive, a spiritual Ecstasy.

I don't understand. Why, after all that happened, did Joana talk to me about the most beautiful night of her life? It "didn't click?" Five fucks, and it "didn't click?" There was love, but not a boner?

What crap is that?

If it had been for real, I told her, we would find that goddamn crush in the pits of hell. But she didn't want it. She said she had puked it all up and been happy. Just like that, and it's all over?

A selfish woman? And I ask myself again, "Was that all?"

Let me think. The shortest and most redundant way to become selfish, and maybe the only way, is to love yourself. At least, the self must be always partying. But if it comes to be that the self, in spite of the enchantment, talent, elegance and all intrinsic qualities, starts grieving, then there's trouble for two reasons.

The first reason is that the selfish person, and I'm talking about Joana here, will necessarily have to ask for the help of other people, antidepressants, the internet, what have you. The second reason is more serious. The person will be struck on the spot they're not at all familiar with—their frailty. At that moment, and because of their fucked-up past (ah, Joana), the selfish person will be inexorably lonely and will pay for their crimes with what they have of most value—the self. And since Joana can't count on herself, I want to tell her that I'm here. I love that girl, even if she is nothing but a selfish broad.

But is this all she is? A selfish broad?

I don't know, I don't know. Oh God, I don't know! Every time I try to understand, things just get worse. For what it's worth, in spite of the deals she made with herself, we still got to this point.

Here, my darling.

Hell is just breaking loose. I think the author of *If This Is a Man* started to kill himself when he started to write his book. To write, I don't know if I've already said this, and if I have, I'll say it again, is a way to kill what's already dead. Therefore, there is nothing better than starting a book, sacrificing the crush. The same crush that Joana confessed she never had on me. There is nothing better than to omit it, to invent another Joana to talk about Joana. "I hope you have enjoyed my little ass." (That was exactly what she wrote in her second e-mail, with the photo of the "little ass" attached).

I loved it, if you want to know. "It was the best little ass I fucked in my life." Is that what you wanted me to write? There, I wrote it. You've got it. Nobody will know the little ass is yours, don't worry. Nobody will know it is you, Natercia.

I JUST WANTED TO GET RID OF THE NIGHT

I made a bet on love (I was an idiot, a fool, I admit) and Joana, the vampire, gave me back a blood clot, and now I agonize inside Joana's night.

The fact is that I've lost or put all my chips on a love that I neglected from the start, and now it's too late. It isn't possible to choose hate to find peace, either. Not even that is possible. Not even that.

Hate, by the way, is just one among the many resources I no longer have. Or it's the only one.

"Maybe one day you'll understand, my love".

If you don't succumb halfway, maybe one day, Joana, you will understand that the curse is giving. You will understand that a curse is able to provoke the most beautiful works of the art of a genius, that it can have as allies the most spectacular destruction tools. One day, Joana, when you have nothing left to destroy, you'll understand what I say, and maybe you'll count on hate to talk about love. But then it may be too late. You'll have lost your most spectacular destruction tools and love will be nothing but a wreck, your last carcass sent back to you. Listen to me, girl!

I have all the right in the world to demand your share. Since now we're made of the same dead souls. If I were in your place, I admit, I would have acted exactly like you, you bitch.

Just to make things clear. I would have kicked my own ass because I love you, and this means nothing, nothing, nothing.

St. John the Baptist Cemetery, my best postcard

The need (need, my ass—in the past I would have called it an itch, now I can't even call it that) to go somewhere after Joana led me, when I lost my identity as a sappy tourist, to a Rio de Janeiro that was imprinted in my Sao Paulo memories, a non-place, lost in the time and space of the biographies written by Ruy Castro, and that, despite everything, came to be again because of Joana, especially after the hug (the first and the last) she gave me before leaving. It was that hug, in front of Lamas, that made the postcard my ultimate destiny.

It is still the same today. I can't leave this sidewalk, this bar. I can't leave her or the city I invented after the end.

I left to look for a Rio full of hills, which is no longer there, and wanted to understand the reason why she abandoned me (I'll never understand) after our chimpanzee night, until dawn, when I still wandered Barata Ribeiro St. boarded the Copacabana-Leblon and passed in front of Serzedelo Correia square, where Clarice Lispector used to feed the pigeons, the same place that Joana had promised me hand-holding and going to the market on weekends.

Ah, Joana. What happened?

Maybe the mixture of wrong time and place made me believe that, beyond the two of us, something was larger than abandonment, it was truly real, and somehow this "something" would support our affair in a place diverse from the misunderstandings we shared... After Joana kicked my ass, the Copacabana-Leblon could have taken me either to "forever" or nowhere...It didn't matter if I arrived at Leblon or got off earlier, on the corner of Maria Quiteria and Prudente de Morais in Ipanema. Joana would be at my side anyway.

She is my guide to this day, especially when I can't get it up, when her ghost appears in spirals. Sometimes I wake up in the middle of the night, thirsty, crying, and Joana is there. So I ask her what happened to us, and she says nothing. She just keeps me company (or watches over me) as if she was saying, "Don't ask me anything, please. I have nothing to say to you".

Ah, Joana. Why?

* * *

So I had unsheltered nostalgia in the city I invented, and I had hangovers that perhaps would make sense if they span in the memory of Vinicius de Moraes or Paulo Mendes Campos, Carlinhos Oliveira or any other writer who had objectively had his ass kicked and lived and were drunk off their asses in a Rio that no longer exists.

Before Joana, I didn't believe in landscapes. I didn't know about the ruins, and in this category I include the chronicles I wrote to nobody, when I was completely shitfaced at Posto Seis, to nobody and to Joana and to the little Indian, our daughter with sad, big eyes, dead the day after. Mother and daughter kept me company in my dreams and scared moments, in distorted time and space. All of this spinning in my head is nothing, or vain satisfactions that I demand from a city that was never mine and owes me nothing (you don't owe me anything either) and that I owe nothing to. My debts, in short, are to myself and to the mistake I made believing in you, my love, and getting here, to this non-place. I don't even know if I can still talk about ruins. Not even that.

I suspect that people invented tourism and the camera with a similar feeling. The difference, in my case, is that the person in the photograph, the posthumous movement and other people's lives are (because of this non-place) my responsibility. For example, I'm sure I'll be taken to São João Batista cemetery when I die. I want to have a cheap novel death, and I have already been keeping eternal company with the Nelson Rodrigues family for a long time. It's more or less like this— I'm dead, and my soul must be very old, so that these certainties are the only things I carry inside me. I made a bet on Joana to escape death, and that's why I suffer so much when I see buildings in construction, recently opened places. Actually, I don't need anything because I don't exist, or I don't have the courage to die again in the same places.

Joana killed me again. I had already lost the enchantment, and lived in a void of pain, agony and perplexity. And now, because of Joana, I had come back to the previous fall. Even after Joana, I have all the elements to wreck and offer myself in sacrifice to the "forever" or "nowhere." But I can't. I wish I could write this—"What really matters to me, after having moved perplexity away, is much more the beauty of contrast than the pain of consummation. I'll face the pit of fire gladly." But I can't. The pain is bigger, Joana.

I wish, as does every ass-kicked idiot, that she could feel my pain, that the feeling of absence had a minimum of reciprocity. But I can't manage even that, wanting. I lack a solid playing hand to bet on and pay for her absence in my life. In my case, it would be almost impossible to think of some hysterical romanticism. To do so, I would have to be the guy I used to be, the guy who used to write for revenge or to get even. That guy disappeared inside of Joana and was fooled.

I don't know if she's having fun right now. Or if she ever had fun on my account. It doesn't matter. I shouldn't suffer and love, not for me, not for Joana. She abandoned me. She returned me to myself, and worse, multiplied by two. But what can I do, if the pain is no longer about me? If I'm not half the man I used to be?

Borges, Poe, Vinicius. Rape. A dream.

I don't know anything anymore. I have nothing left of Joana. I can't even ask for the benefit of doubt. "Don't ask me why," is what she says, again and again. Joana is my "Nevermore raven," without a single construction of intelligence to explain her.

It's curious, in the beginning of Poe's famous poem, as told by Jorge Luis Borges, the author of "The Murders in the Rue Morgue" believed that the most memorable, efficient characters in the English language were "o" and "r". So, he stumbled into the expression "Nevermore" and repeated it continuously. Simple, isn't it?

Rudimentary, I would say. I say it, but not to be taken for granted. My intention here is to confront Poe's raven with the foot that kicked my ass. I can quietly declare that Joana is the raven that Poe could never see, simply because neither he nor Borges had the love (or the bad luck) to be able to. Instead of repeating "nevermore" incessantly, the woman who promised me a life of simple things, tax-paying and children enrolled in private schools, repeats, "Don't ask me why." Worst of all, she's alive and has a soft skin, whereas Lenore, Poe's lost lover, has simply kicked the bucket and is only a phantasmagoric echo reproduced by a raven that could very well be a parrot. On the other hand, it's as if I couldn't enjoy life and death didn't exist, and these two "states," let's put it this way, were my interlocutors at the same time. Where do I stand? This is the question Poe asked himself, "Where does the lover stand?"

The choice, an obvious one, for it was a poem after all, was to contrast the raven's blackness to the paleness of Palas Atenas's bust. So, Poe decided to stick the inconsolable lover in a library and wins Borges over. What is a library? It is a refuge, where supposedly the books come to the aid of the desperate lover, in contrast to life and death. Worst of all, if the help of knowledge weren't enough (this is the thesis), the structure of the poem itself would ensure an answer (or desired whip), blind and final, that is, eternity—very convenient to Borges, by the way.

In a last analysis, the raven is a construction of Poe's intelligence, duly minimized by Borges. Or would it be right to say smartly minimized by Borges? Who, using it to his own advantage, writes the following, "the man knows that he's sentenced to spend the rest of his life, of his *fantastic* life, talking to the raven, which will always say 'nevermore.'" At this point, the Argentinian surreptitiously abandons the idea that a life can be "fantastic" if ignored due to the denial of itself. Only if it was his life, Borges' life, who, besides being blind and a misogynist, was a genius who could defend and disguise his shortcomings like nobody else, as if he was defending the very notion of art.

* * *

Whether it's truly art or a mere shortcoming, it doesn't matter to me. I don't accept it. I don't want this shit. Maybe what happened was that I didn't have the time for disappointment. One night was too much. Joana must be nuts to have involved herself in that story.

Her mother hung herself at thirty-one and her father used emotional blackmail, as well as showed some obvious attraction towards Joana. A rape story is part of the nightmare that she had started to reveal to me, little by little, during the phone calls that lasted for the whole night and early morning. She called me to tell me who she was, as long as I didn't ask her "Why?"

* * *

When she was thirteen, she lived in Nigeria. She became a young woman there. Her father, besides being a poet, was an engineer with Acquaservice, one of the Brazilian companies hired by the Nigerian military government. In Lagos, she started to notice the existence of men. And the existence of boys, but boys had interests that were way too pragmatic compared to her interests at that time. "They were so innocent." She didn't know what it was at the time, but she felt some kind of itch, and the first signs of the clairvoyance that always showed her "the opposite thing." At 13, she preferred impossible men. That was when Vinicius de Moraes came into her life. Vinicius was the soundtrack in the streets of Lagos, in the car's cassette player. "Oh, my beloved, what eyes you have/ they are night ports, full of goodbyes/ they're soft docks/ trailing lights/ shining in the distance/ far into the darkness/ so much mystery/ in your hair/ so many sailboats/ so many ships/ so many wrecks/ in these eyes of yours."

Joana wanted to love like that, and her desire sailed on those songs. It was so shameless that once, out of the blue, her stepmother said to her, "He's old enough to be your father!" She was talking about one of Joana's father's friends, a funny, bohemian young man who wore a beard and whom she had fallen in love with. Ah, so many boats, so many ships, so many wrecks. Joana found the warning weird. She thought that what she felt was a secret. And because the warning came together with an unreasonable, noisy anger, Joana didn't hear the mix of jealousy, envy and contempt in the voice of her father's wife.

Back in Brazil, her father, as a poet, told her about life one day, in the backyard of the family home. He had never talked like that before. "I dreamed of children. I dreamed of a house and a garden." What that man told her, Joana confessed to me, didn't sound like her father. "Not like that." He was regretful. Joana also had to deal with the excess of novelty when her poet father started a new subject. "A friend of mine, the CEO of our company, made love to his fifteen-year-old daughter." It was her father's first verse.

Joana didn't know if she'd answered him, or if she'd dreamt of her father's proposal. She remembered her childhood home like a movie—four windowed doors opening to the backyard. The house, her father and the pain she felt from the madman's speech passed by her as if the girl had been on the edge of an eclipse for all those years. In the background— the last door was the one to her father and stepmother's room. Joana entered the house through that door, crossed the corridor and ended up in the front, on a street bathed in sunshine. It was a dark house and it wasn't the dramatic love she desired. Vinicius, Joana told me, saved her from loving her father. The poet made her age without noticing, and, as far as she knew, would protect her youth forever.

* * *

Oh God! Why?

I strangled my days asking, "Why?" I was sure that the boner was the least important thing, and that having deposited my spunk inside her had been the bravest, most decent thing I had perpetrated in the last thirty years. So what?

She told me she would suffer a lot if she had to commit some kind of violence against herself. That consoled me, somehow, because I was responsible, too. The morning after pill altered her moods and gave her acne.

Was that all? She preferred to believe she had lost nothing. What a wise cow. There's no denying that. If I could choose the violence Joana would commit against herself, I'd rather, let's say, have actually gotten her pregnant. I don't know. It would be a way to bring a child into the game, or something less fluid and passionate than my spunk—dead flesh inside of a dead soul. Joana surely deserved that.

On the other hand, we gained, gained too much, in confidence. Never before had a woman trusted me so much. All the others (either in cash or installments) I'd had cut in half, always wearing a condom, duly protected. Not Joana. She was with me until the end, and, looking back, she was the first woman with whom I had something to share, even though that "something" had supposedly never existed, even though we'd killed the little Indian, that little something, or nothing, together.

Two days after the chimpanzee night

We arranged to meet for dinner for the second-to-last time, and then I was ass-kicked. She took the initiative. She called my hotel and suggested a barbecue place in Copacabana. I could only believe her. Me, the one who never believed in love and orgasms. "I'll be waiting at nine, sweetheart."

At nine. Yes, of course.

It is worth it to say that our foul mischance was so perfect that besides giving spiral kisses, my sweet beloved also devoured liver steaks and gizzards with onions, sure of something I had yet to understand. It wasn't the meat or the two of us, but the already mentioned foul mischance.

Anyway, even though I didn't understand a thing, I had the impression that I had lost her several times during the meal. The first time was because of the way Joana swallowed the pork rib, without noticing my astonishment, and because of her insensibility, dismissing the protocol of side dishes. The girl was more in a hurry than hungry, and we sat apart at the table. The strangest thing was that I liked her attitude. The distance between us was, in my guess, an old way of getting closer. It was as if, evidently in spite of my shock and Joana's indifference, we knew each other too well to ignore the appropriate procedures and gestures expected from a couple of lovers, including my shock and her indifference.

It was a true marriage, in this case, that failed to happen at the right time. Let us say that the disinterest, and the love, and the meat served on a stick, could feel like fifty years in two and a half hours of estrangement and mutual empathy.

It was not a case of saying that the attraction could have been replaced by prime ribs or a juicy piece of meat with garlic, or anything like that. Technically, "it would not the case," but that was what happened. I lost my appetite. And I changed seats. After all, we did the deed in mutual agreement. I was duly fueled by Viagra and she was running away from my French kisses.

Joana turned away from me twice. The abortion did not have, for her, the same romantic characteristics that I attributed to it, in spite of the meal. That, and the morning-after pill and the internet pranks etc., messed with her moods (she had thrown up the next day, as she made sure to repeat between rare steaks). And as for me, well, I thought everything was beautiful, mainly the way Joana handled her cutlery and how she called to the waiter. Even today, I still don't have the eyes to see things differently, and any aggression invariably enchants me. It doesn't matter if it came from her, the cutlery or the waiter serving us. I suspect the best word to describe the infatuated state I was and am in is "unsuspecting." Trying to disqualify her because of the way she acted is nonsense. The opposite is pure enchantment. Then, I would be lying if I said I wasn't happy and I hadn't noticed the main thing—I had been kicked in the ass. So, was that all?

The mix of hormones and mammalian complications, everything they make sure to demand and emphasize regarding the complexity of their bodies and minds, was all that insignificant enough to be thrown up like that? Or bled every month? Including the love of the idiot who paid half of the restaurant bill?

Joana threw me up. In short, that was what she told me and then untold me, the whole time, that is, if I understood things properly. When we were paying the bill, she made sure to give me back the taxi money, the money I had lent her after our chimpanzee night, and thought that it was okay, thought it was fair.

That meant Joana had another fellow besides her favorite writer, with whom she shared expenses and vomited excesses. And this fellow couldn't hold her hand, simply because it slipped away.

What the hell had happened? Rio de Janeiro wouldn't serve as my scenery, wouldn't I have even that?

I no longer understood a thing. Not after the steak house in Copacabana. The truth was that I had never known anything about women, except, of course, about their genitalia, and I didn't mind paying their taxi fare. It is also true that no woman had ever waved me goodbye, throwing me a kiss before leaving, like we were in a movie. No one like Joana.

Love, for me, was still the same wrong bus, boarding at Flamengo and getting off in Leblon without noticing Copacabana in the middle. If, before Joana, it was already difficult for me to understand my itinerary or "my place in this world," then after her and her abysses, which were nothing but narrow streams of water and the little madness controlled with violent medication, and the children killed the morning after, and even the beauty disguised as tragedy, and that was more beautiful, more tragic because of it, well, in short, if before her and this package of novelties and cemeteries it was difficult for me to cross streets and say good morning to the doorman, then after her I lost my sense of navigation completely, as well as what little I had left of what people call "one's self," or of the fellow who (before, before that woman) could find himself despite the chaos, even though "he" was the same person and, in one way or another, could arrive late to the wrong places.

Now, I don't even have that. Besides myself, I have Joana to lose. And she threw me up the next day, with grace and no ceremony.

* * *

Impeccable and a total bitch. Reckless and selfish, as if under a spell. As if, due to the absence of her suicidal mother, she could pamper herself in a diabolical blindfold game downhill. And she invited me to the game, and then dismissed me.

* * *

The day after the barbecue restaurant, Joana called my hotel and said she needed to talk to me. We were still a couple of chimpanzees.

So, I called her three times to tell her I'd get to the meeting place early and it didn't matter if she took an hour to come. Where?

"On the corner of Santa Clara and Atlântica. Easy, my love. I'll just take a shower and will be there in fifteen minutes."

After two hours, she showed up and I didn't recognize her. I had no courage to ask her for a kiss (or a discount?). Joana's hair was wet. Maybe she has another guy. Maybe she spent the night taking drugs. The sure thing was that her voice had changed and she was wearing a worn-out pair of sneakers, and one of them had a hole. I was the same man. My body pissed on the wall and words blocked my esophagus. I couldn't say anything and now I'm alone in Rio de Janeiro. Something tells me Joana is a lesbian and I strangely remember all my late rental bills. Not to mention that just a week before I was exposing myself unnecessarily on the internet, offering the silliest excuses to be publicly ridiculed, and enjoyed it. She was hungry, and, once again, I didn't know what to do. We walked, and I told her I had spent the night reading and writing, locked in my hotel room thinking of her, that my beard was grey and my body was flaccid. She was twenty-one.

That didn't matter, she declared. My flaccid body and our age difference didn't mean a thing. It was written on her (our?) astral map, according to a clairvoyant, her friend, our time had come.

To help me relax, she ordered two beers.

"Let's talk, my love."

Yes, yes. Let's talk. I explained that the man who fucked her five times was the writer, and that apart from Viagra, I had nothing to do with him. Of course, I was better than the son-of-a-bitch she imagined burning her ass with cigarette butts or slapping her hard. I was better than that sadistic idiot, because I was there, two days later, totally in love and thinking of justifications or diagnostics that she, the reader, already knew and probably offered in a double dose. Maybe I'd even forget about the burning and slapping to begin with, because I had no need to justify myself to her, and also because the book guy had retreated at the dawn of the perfect night and visibly abandoned me, and her, without paying the bill, and we tried (I tried harder than her) to negotiate (with whom?) without further damage. At that point, I told her about Viagra.

"I already knew that, honey. I'm totally in favor of the pharmaceutical industry."

And then, with the same sleepy inflexion, she told me something about her carioca nights, something about a Frenchman with a name that sounded like red wine, who had fucked her twice and disappeared, someone named Chevalier, I think.

I didn't know what to do, although I played the son-of-a-bitch better than him, and in spite of being responsible for him and for the excitement that we had lost together at the barbecue place the day before, I didn't know what to do.

"I think you should calm down, my love."

One beer after another.

"No one has fooled anyone." That's what she said to me.

That was the worst thing. There was no fraud to explain our mismatch. Only the mismatch itself. And two more days at the hotel, waiting for a phone call.

I decided to wait until Wednesday. Thursday, at most. I still preferred to believe the lie. I included Joana. Or I invented myself to fit the invention, which, at the end of the day, was her. So, it wasn't a lie, but, I want to believe, some gadget that served me well and, according to my calculations, useful to dodge her negatives on the phone and to meet my most delirious expectations, as the certainty that such inclusion was some kind of promise of metaphysical masturbation she was still about to "enjoy," even more than the hand job that would effectively serve me, and fail me. So, the wait that should have disappointed me brought me closer to Joana. I invested my sperm in it, my love, a promise of who knows what, or what could have been and was not. The excitement, one that I had nothing to do with, had lied, had killed the love.

Therefore, don't let sexual excitement kill love, Joana. Don't joke. You told me you wanted to have a lot of children, that we'd get married, that the goddamn clairvoyant and the fucking astral map had confirmed everything. As the older guy, you told me to come, and I am here, I have traveled for forty years only to fuck you. Don't leave me, don't kill me, don't do this, because I'm not some son-of-a-bitch who wanted only to fuck you and call you a bimbo. This doesn't matter to me at all. Come on, you have killed what never existed, but now you want to kill me with tomorrow and you will kill me the day after tomorrow and the next week. Yes, I'll leave. But I'll die day after day. And the other day was me, unhappened. Don't do this. I've never had a woman who'd smeared herself with lipstick and taken pictures naked for me. Don't leave me. No other woman has ever shaved her pussy in the old-fashioned way just to wait for me. You told me you'd wait for me at the motel, drunk on whiskey, and the clairvoyant and the astral maps and the arousal and all the fucking bullshit. And now all this can't possibly kill love, can it? Do you understand? Don't leave me so soon. Just once, after forty years, is nothing for someone who has waited all his life to hear what you said to me. Ah, Joana, I don't want to swallow your morning-after pill. Don't kill me. Don't be like this. Listen, yesterday I published a chronicle, and I spent the whole afternoon being insulted on the internet because I dedicated the text to you. I dared to say that people made a circus out of Chico Buarque's book and that no one would ever force me to like my assailants' soundtrack, because, among other aberrations, I love you and I mixed it all up just to repeat your name. Rio de Janeiro and my love mean nothing without you. No, without you I could be anywhere, without you there are no landscapes. Do you understand? I can't see how you could kill the landscapes from the outside, and at the same time be happy for the simple fact of living alone, and throw me up as if I were another Frenchmen with a red wine name. See, that was a mistake. He disappeared, and I was just another bottle in your wine cellar. And now I'm here, half-dead, going through all the motions, walking the ridiculous *via crucis* the day after. And maybe I'm still stuck on the first sweet station of my stupid hell, waiting for you. Shit, why does it have to be like this? I have lost my best pretexts, and I don't know what to say. Actually, I don't want this anymore. There's no sense in calling you "my bimbo." I feel ridiculous serving you and your sexual desire, and I'm leaving Rio de Janeiro first thing tomorrow. I have traveled all this time, I lost myself and I blew it all because of this goddamn foul mischance you invented with me to destroy me once more, and now I write and write, and everyone, including you and me, believes what I say and replicates my fuck up as if it were, ah, as if it were their own. Ah, call me. I can't be more of a hick and predictable than a goddamn silent phone, and love stories are like this anyway, and my style is already compromised, and fuck my style because I love you and will love you anyway, despite the failure written on the palm of my hand that you read with such curiosity and premeditation. And I fell into all of your traps willingly, as if I had invented them myself. Oh, my love, give me a sign, come use me and throw me away again, because you know I do everything wrong and have no control, you know you can kill me as many times as you please, and I have lost my nerve. And although I'm no longer the guy who wrote the books, I bear some resemblance to the son-of-a-bitch whom you imagined burning your soft, round ass with cigarette butts. If things can be reduced to these terms, your terms, oh, my love, ah, Joana, call me and say no. I can still pretend I'm bad if it makes you happy, and somehow help with the creation of a foul mischance which is more ridiculous than your imminent fantasy. I will pretend, it is no problem, my love. I will burn your whole body and lick your asshole and you will kill me in the morning and I will leave and you will kill me again. It doesn't matter. But give me a sign and call me, you cold, indifferent, crazy bitch. You killer, love of my life. Ah, Joana, maybe I'll change time zones for you and write another book in spite of myself. You know, my bimbo, if this is the case (once again, once again) I will go through all the stations of love to lose you in the morning. I don't care, that is, unless at this very moment you are sucking in spirals a cock that's not mine. If you throw it all up tomorrow, I don't care, you see? Listen to me, the certainty or uncertainty that you might have about "our love" won't change the damned result of all this—a book. Was this what you wanted, a book? If that was all, my love, you got it, and I will use your name as many times as I find necessary, because I don't want this book. It's yours. And I will talk about you and "our intimacy" in spite of you and in spite of myself. Of course I will. It's the only chance I have. Because, if you have been worried about "intimacies," well, this means we had something. And it was exactly this "something" that I didn't notice or couldn't identify when I zigzagged from Aterro do Flamengo to Marina da Glória. And it was this something that made me feel no longer a foreigner, and the scenery was you and my love, you and our mismatched intimacies. I'd say we had more complicity than desire. And there's more—the perspective that arousal would ask for a truce calmed me a lot. Ah, I was a fool. I recognize it. You know, Joana, I don't need the excitement anymore. I would just call for my friends' help and ask them for some two thousand bucks so I could spend a few more nights with you, and we could repeat that cold beer kiss, and toast to our lack of desire together. I mean, I think so, maybe. Oh God! My God! Why?

A KICK IN THE ASS

And she called the hotel. I didn't understand what was happening to us after our chimpanzee night. I don't know. Joana must have been preparing the farewell scene, and she surely knew we would cry together, she, more than I, when she finally announced that everything had been a mistake. That desire (the unhappened desire), the goddamn cinematographic-literary desire, the subgenre she would use so well from the first email (with my help, of course) until the final kick in the ass at the Arabian restaurant, had defeated love.

* * *

I was eating a lamb kafta, and really took pity on both of us. I somehow took more pity on her, because I could remember my *modus operandi* in my twenties. Joana used my own methods and made sure to sneak away from love, and throw into the garbage bin whatever garbage there was. It was simple and predictable—Joana was lonely. And she would suffer with that. My loneliness. Perhaps that was why I cried with her, as if I was crying for my own wasted time, in a ridiculous attempt to redeem myself—ridiculous, because it was the time of my life, and even more ridiculous because Joana was as manipulative as I could ever be, or even more, despite the books I've written and mainly because I have never had a pussy between my legs. Ah, such delight.

The truth is that I've always had the habit of exaggerating. I've always been an inventor of spiritual Viagras, a foreteller of unhappenings. Sometimes I could even convince myself of that, and could, and still can, persuade myself, or conciliate the inconciliable. I used to mix, and still mix, this and that and, if I didn't watch myself closely, there would have been only three possible results. I would have gone mad, or, I don't know, I would have invented some new psychoanalysis, with a funnier, wilder expiration date. Or, to be more realistic, what happened would still have happened. I would have lost my temper, as I did, and kept standing firmly on Joana's ground. This is how, after the kick in the ass, events started having a stronger, more beautiful relevance for me than they really deserved. It couldn't be any different.

As I've said, maybe Joana was only trying to get to places I've never reached. I am taking into account all of the time lost, all of the souls disposed after use, and the morning that I woke up in an empty parking lot in Santa Catarina, half-drunk and sure I had been brutally murdered despite the fog that softly kissed the sands of the Cabeçudas beach.

I want to say that Joana's chances of reaching places I've never reached were evidently bigger and more compromising than mine, due to the traits of her sex.

But in this case, my exaggeration would be easily explained, mainly because of her unmeasured generosity. For she fucked me without asking for a condom, and with the goddamn suicidal desire we anticipated in and invented for each other. The problem was that we included love in the mix, or better, we made a bet, or at least I did. And we bet all our golden chips on the most difficult thing as if it were the easiest.

Why love, when we had all the rest? If Joana had read

all my books, and we were so alike, why waste time with love? That would come naturally. It was part of the tacit package of lascivious acts with the pussy she had shaved especially for me, the five shots of whiskey she swallowed while waiting for me to arrive, the clairvoyant, the astral maps, our rising signs and her lipstick-smeared mouth. Why love, if we had so much? We had an old motel in Largo do Machado and each other. She was the twenty-year-old pussycat and I was her favorite writer. "Fuck me, you're the best writer in Brazil," that was the first thing I heard from her. Why love?

"I'll wait for you drunk on whiskey, and not another word. Enough flicking the bean, enough hand jobs. On the 18th, at midnight, my love."

Why love, if, among other more useful and useless things she or it (desire? a spiritual entity? a demon?) was also there in that motel room to steal my sperm? When I believed that love didn't need a messenger, or anything but love itself to exist, whatever.

I was a fool, I recognize that. I blew it. Joana and I cried together as if she could see the briefness of our encounter, and I, in spite myself, was playing the demon that possessed her. For what? Perhaps to prove that in spite of the fiasco, and "for the first time," I had learned to love and was grateful to Joana, and had my own tricks?

I sincerely don't know. I offered her a piece of the lamb kafta and she squeezed my hand, and then Joana laid down on my lap and told me the truth as if it was a lie. It would be difficult, not to mention dishonest, to say that that girl was only an expert in manipulating others, or that she had fun with her own desire, or that she solved her problems with the morning-after pill. I prefer to believe that Joana was a great woman. And that I lost her.

BEFORE

I'm glad everything happened in Rio. She chose the place—Hotel Serrano in Largo do Machado. June 18th, at midnight. "I'll wait for you drunk on whiskey." Great, we had a deal. Joana also promised me that tiny black thong, the one from the first photograph sent by email.

My conditions—no more photographs, no more phone calls, no more emails. I arrived at these terms after Joana had sent me her thighs and her feet. I had already bought the whole package, accepting the risk that she could have an ugly face. That is, the beautiful ass in the first picture, the firm thighs, followed by the tanned shoulders and the breasts with pink nipples were enough to calm me down, and for some reason I decided not to ask for a picture of her face, knowing for sure that she was very beautiful. I knew that more because of tactics than intuition. If I didn't ask to see her face, I would show confidence, and she would feel more desired and pretty. And even if she was ugly, I had decided that she would become beautiful. The last email she sent came with a photo of her pussy, shaved in a conservative cut, "especially for you." Oh, oh. For me.

Let's say that the package, or the Joana who came with that pussy, deserved my detachment. Before I speak of our encounter, however, I want to say something about the phone calls. I noticed, if this is possible, since the first time we spoke, a tone of voice that was oscillating, hoarse, with a soft carioca accent, almost sleepy. Joana had just turned twenty-one and had been in Rio for the last three months, running away from a weird marriage. Something to do with a carioca Jew from the countryside of the United States. When she said, "I've been married" or "I've lived with a guy," and said she couldn't think of husband and wife living in separate places, I had the conviction that she was anticipating our own marriage, and saw myself in the place of the carioca Jew doing some stupid job in Texas, always fearing being discovered by immigration officers. All of a sudden, it was as if we had been married since the first phone call.

I jerked off a lot because of this "inclusion." An honest, unprecedented thing.

It was different from the other times, when I got off thinking only of my sexual obsessions. For the first time, I was thinking about a real woman, and I was the man attached to my own dick. When I beat off for Joana, it had nothing to do with those libido Frankensteins I had gotten used to throughout the years. I dare say it was an almost Catholic jacking off.

Or else it was because I had never, at any moment in my life, let myself be "included" in anything. It would be very easy to say I had chosen to be solitary. But that's not all. Maybe I didn't even suspect my own independence, and wasn't fragile enough to be afraid of failure. I mean, I always kept myself to myself. I kept the appropriate distance and missed the best opportunities deliberately. Therefore, this is not only about a guy who has never had a little woman, it's about a guy who's always had some autonomy and freedom, acquired through premeditated distance. I chose my losses myself, and chose to be alone. The acts of grandeur, as well as the acts of misery, were intrinsic. With that, I developed a thick skin that protected me from reality and gave me strength to move forward, apart from everything and everyone. In these conditions, I would never think of sharing my desires with a little woman, not that I didn't trust myself and know myself enough to realize I was uptight, much to the opposite. The problem, let's say, was that women didn't have the tools. They didn't know how to face me and my forbidden, weird independence. I was a great wanker. From then on, the easiest solution regarding women was to devour them. Literally, I became a ridiculous cannibal of souls, a charming, stylish stray dog.

Mea culpa. Following this train of thought, I have always despised the meat and the souls offered to me, using them and then throwing them away. I sincerely thought that life wasn't worth living. So, for me, it was very easy to kill all commonplaces and write five brilliant books. Now, all is explained. I did the most obvious, redundant, selfish thing. I exchanged life for art.

Until Joana came. She included me. The goddamn bitch told me life was bigger. Oh God. She was bluffing, "Fuck me, you're the greatest writer in Brazil," and using my own weapons!

Well, I accepted. I said "I love you," and I knew happiness and all the commonplaces I had rejected, and I believed in fucking life, sharing all the mammalian fluids and Mexican food. As if that wasn't enough, Joana quoted excerpts from my books and wanted to have three children, all boys, with me. I negotiated for a little girl, who would always be my favorite, and we also talked about dogs and cats, and she said she'd go with me anywhere, and even when we hung up the telephone we exchanged shy sweetheart goodbyes and kisses that had nothing to do with the lack of control of the emails. The next day, the phone call was equally as embarrassing and delicate, both on her part, who wanted to know my date of birth and insisted on that Mexican food shit, and on my part, who had trouble saying I had been born on May 9th, 1964, and yes, I liked Mexican food and any food she liked. And, I wasn't sure, but I thought that my rising sign, which was something she wanted to know about, was Scorpio or something like that, and there was a place where my path would meet hers in the Mars sky or wherever. And we stammered on the phone and said goodbye with "a big kiss" and "millions of kisses for you." For me, millions of kisses for me. Oh God.

The next day, I saw Joana's face. I didn't ask, but she sent me a photo by email. She was really beautiful, with big hazel eyes and a mouth full of lipstick, which she intended to use "to give me millions of kisses." My God, me, someone who had spent most of his life licking bathroom tiles and using the most improbable places in my libido to draw out some sperm to the point of exhausting it, as if this was possible. Oh God. "Millions of kisses" to an uptight man, who had spent his life collecting abysses and, above all, making all efforts to avoid and repel the proximity with anything but the abyss itself. Was it desire or disease? It didn't matter. What mattered was that I was self-sufficient enough and managed to contaminate my surroundings, and I fed on this, and destroyed to create, and everything could just be empty and start from a simple, pro-verbial hand job. Kisses, I miss you.

She was in Rio de Janeiro and I had spent forty years nowhere, running away from her. On June 8th, 2004, after 130 years, Venus eclipsed the Sun and I didn't see any use in astro-logical meteorology, or couldn't (although I had already start-ed to believe in coincidences) replace the image of the eclipse with the pictures of Joana, which were more and more porno-graphic. I mean, I jerked off a lot because of astral movements and especially with the picture of Joana's round belly, the same belly I had idealized that I would rest my head on, after all of the fights and so much time lost in self-abusing. I even started to believe that I had "wasted time" jerking off. One thing had nothing to do with the other. Well, was Venus a sign? Oh, fuck off. Fuck it.

What used to be jerking off became destiny, and my desire, in a strange way, followed the movement of the planets, foretelling doom.

According to Joana's astral studies (via email, attached with a picture of her exfoliating her heels), I could easily replace George Bush as head of the American government and do a very good job. I had real possibilities of invading Iran and North Korea and destroying the whole world, so strong was my selfishness and my eagerness for despising other people's feelings. Bull's eye. That's what she saw on my astral map. Our desire, however, was such that Joana found a way to cross our data, pirouette around Jupiter and put Venus up her ass to match my crazy rising signs. Now, it was confirmed. Taurus, Taurus and Capricorn evidently matched horns and her own star sign. We were made for each other, and if that wasn't enough, Joana was in her fertile time. She was "mad" to see me, and besides a sky full of stars in our favor, she included a clairvoyant friend who had told her there would be an older, famous man in her life, a perfect man. I was indeed older, and I could become famous anytime, and would gladly trade all my future fame for the cooked rice she had sworn was her specialty. We would go together to the beach and my favorite daughter would be called Ritinha, even if she didn't like it. And we had a deal. June 18th, midnight, at Hotel Serrano. Great. After forty years, I had found my Eva Braun. What I couldn't have imagined was that, truly, we had arranged our end.

The picture of her shaved pussy, "just for you, my love," (a conservative cut, for me) made me repeat my previous request—our meeting had to happen on neutral ground, in Rio de Janeiro. Let's stop with the emails and phone calls.

She said yes, she accepted.

Once more, drunk on whiskey, mouth smeared with lipstick. I would show up with a thick beard, fat, and would "do her" starting from her ass, as per irrevocable astral requests. That was all right with me. Without a condom was even better.

Fertile time. Oh, oh.

On Valentine's' Day, June 12^{th3}, I called her. It was the first time I'd done that. It was Valentine's Day, and Joana was getting ready for the most important night of her life, waiting for me. She invented two other children and a Labrador, and sheets hung to dry on the backyard. I think that was all.

There were six days to go. The excitement of the wait bothered me (it was growing in itself, I could say). I decided to routinely jack off, without thinking of Joana, and following only the demands of the Gregorian calendar I had. Time was taking too long to pass. This was reflected in the email I sent when there were five days to go. I was laconic, but I couldn't help showing interest. I knew she would react accordingly. And once more Joana surprised me. She said she had also "jerked off for me," and told me to stop being silly and "flick my bean for her." Ah, Joana.

I imagined that starting the emails with "my darling," or any other "my this or that" would somehow ensure my virility in advance, as if I was marking my territory. I don't know. I had become almost a little monkey, acting out of instinct and sense of smell. For a long time, since my long forgotten beach soccer with the guys, I had stopped practicing those things.

"Darling…"

Perhaps I acted like that so I wouldn't remember the passing of the years, or even to expurgate those tactile, wild times—Oh, how I miss those times—when I didn't know how to cut a deck of cards and used my intelligence to escape from myself or simply forget the loving feeling and suffocate it, putting it in its appropriate drawer, saving it for a distant, very

---

3 Editors' note: June 12th is Brazilian Valentine's Day

distant future. Ah, I had my future under control, as if I didn't need any foretelling skills and solitude had chosen me in a cheating move, before Joana. Distance would protect me from the future, and I would never care about waiting and suffering. Those were times when, despite the punishments and the fear and the unknown, despite everything and myself, I managed to be happy with so little, happy with myself.

It was exactly this feeling that impregnated me once again. This time, however, for such an improbable, unhappened reason as the beach soccer fields of my pre-adolescence—the love of a little woman. From that moment on, my solitude was over. I believed I could free myself from the desert, that Joana's company was more trustworthy than my own, and that I could move forward, with her, she and I, two chimpanzees. And it was really good.

Joana responded with little games, sweethearts' foolishness, embarrassing delights—when seen from the outside I can only call them Honey. It was, actually, a whole itinerary of obvious delicate moves and promises of rides, tickles and an infinity of caresses and nicknames which, today, I try to avoid, but have no way of saying "this isn't ridiculous," simply because it is really ridiculous, but necessary. Ask any FM radio station, they live on this. With Joana, it wouldn't be any different. I would recover all time lost, of course. I believed this. I believed that she was part of my oldest undoings. And, even during the wait, well, I had made an effort for her and for the first time invented carnivals, *pierrots* and columbines. And there was more. Because of our love, I was happy and knew the sticky trance of the infatuated, including unsuspected bouts of jealousy & supernatural coincidences, tacit demands and kisses, children, duvets, dogs and cats. Everything about Joana enchanted me, and she returned my feelings, saying, yes, "covered with lipstick, my love." And, finally the time came to listen to Roberto Carlos, trust clairvoyants and foretellers, smell the ocean, ride and be ridden (in the strict sense, of course). The situation was under control!

Oh God, I believed so!

The most intriguing thing is that, even though I had "the situation under control," I never ceased to meet the sweetest, affectionate, mammalian expectations, all on her part. The strongest proof of my craziness (or coherence?) was that I immediately accepted her marriage proposal. I had no doubts at all. I mean, I won't lie, it was obvious that the manipulator knew he was being manipulated. So what?

I continued, in my imagined prudence, using tender nicknames, going crazy with the explicit photographs she kept sending me by email, and jerking off to make fun of astral conjunctions without suspecting that the preposterous situation was, in truth, a diabolical cocktail mixer that blended desire and tenderness, two explosive feelings, irreconcilable for me before. Fuck. Fuck. It was a fucking mess, the type of senseless, crazy, improbable thing that was out of my reach and beyond the usual *hors d'ouevres*.

I was aware that the only thing I could do was blow it, which, I should say, didn't mean much when it came to a man in love for the first time. "Awareness," in this case, was something very close to "total lack of choices," or sheer blindness. Or lightness, that's it, lightness. That was exactly what I felt when I imagined Joana, and myself, in a Roberto Carlos' song. The image of "breakfast in bed for two" and a second-rate motel was recurring and made me anxious.

The fact that I had never believed in "breakfast in bed for two," and all that corny astrological bullshit (now denied), didn't at all mean that Joana couldn't also disbelieve, and consequently wasn't giving more reins to this wild horse she was mounting. Looking back, it couldn't have been any different. Both Joana and I only needed one thing among all that—Roberto Carlos. Or worse—the game. And Joana knew how to bluff. She used my declared fetishes against me and seduced me with my own deteriorated repertoire.

It was an evident trap, set by myself, which I fell into by pretending. For I've never believed anything I've written. She did. She believed, and she wanted to fuck me. This is why I can't say we lied to each other, but we created a fiction, she, more than me. My fiction, the poison I'd produced, the demon I'd invented from the beginning could only come from my most beautiful debris to which I hadn't paid any attention to anyway, until Joana came.

Two days to go till our meeting

Joana would smoke Gauloises naked, and told me something that sounded like "drowsiness," at least I think so, and she made the reservations for the seedy hotel herself, informing me that she would wear black panties to wait for me. And she did more. A week before the date, she slept for a night in our suite and took several photographs of her naked body, multiplied many times by the countless mirrors on the walls. She sent the pictures by email.

"Not even Borges would have dreamt of these labyrinths." That was the email subject. She also said she had learned to enjoy sushi and that she had come from my rib.

If that had been the case, I would learn to eat Japanese food with hashi. I wanted all commonplaces for myself. It wasn't a matter of taking it easy. It was a matter of desire. A desire of the corrupted type, of someone who jerks off thinking of Fatima Bernardes doing a Christmas special report, or who, like myself, had never participated in a game of Secret Santa. It was a matter of inclusion, just as I said.

Well, on June 18th I received my paycheck and my plan was to squander it all with Joana. I took the first plane. I arrived in Rio de Janeiro at four in the afternoon. I familiarized myself with the area and couldn't decide whether to buy

Viagra or not. I was ashamed.

I was afraid I wouldn't be up to it, that I wouldn't be enough for the ingenious, totally crazy pussycat called Joana, my love.

I bought the little blue pill, despite my embarrassment. Anyhow, I had decided to divide my life in two periods—before and after Joana. I took my post at the Adega do Portuga, a bar in Largo do Machado. I thought of my friends and foes, and wrote the next week's chronicle, asking for retraction from the writers who had won the Jabuti awards and monthly scholarships when it was I who deserved them all for *The Blue of the Deceased Son* (cash deposits are welcome at Itaú bank, branch number 0189, account 48227-6).

"To compensate for the biggest negligence in the history of Brazilian literature, waiter, I would like a beer."

Despite everything, I am a Christian. And before I say anything else, Mr. Waiter, I want to make things very clear. I've always been a lonely guy. I have recently made a lot of new friends, and developed a deep affection (maybe too deep) for many people who I would never have imagined as friends.

"Maybe too deep," because, besides being lonely, I had never needed anyone to tell me I am an idiot because of this or that. I know myself well. I know the shortcomings I carry here and there in M.M. form. Maybe I know them better than myself, and, what is worse, I have the conviction that it is worth it to develop "affection" for (to give credit) and to become closer to these shortcomings, especially to that someone and their cheeky, sad sophisms. If not by affinity, at least to avoid the embarrassment of having their work compared to mine. Do you get the message? If you didn't feel uncomfortable with that, eternity will make sure all deposits are made. I don't think there is any need for another parenthesis.

And there's one more thing. From the knowledge of the subject in question, I have also acquired a double ability to detect and regret the affection that people have mistakenly given me. Montaigne would be jealous. This, I think it's easy to notice, is not the kind of literature written by someone who would set fire to their own clothes. It is, above all else, a love story, apparently under control.

The problem is that I feel touched by my friends and foes. I would kill and die in the name of a Chicabon ice lolly, and I demand the same sacrifice. Meaning my position is consummated and it goes only until the point that pleases me.

"One more beer, waiter."

So, I don't have to punish myself, or convince anyone to buy my goods. I have my own means and liturgies, and I demand, I repeat, the counterpart. I am able (or was, before Joana) to consume, among other banalities and in the name of a friendship, several six packs, or even to spend the whole afternoon laughing at other people's jokes just to forget that the real background has always been and will always be my interest in myself.

"One Steinhaeger. And another beer."

What matters, at the end of the day, is (or was) my loneliness, or my lack of interest. I mean, I took things as they came, and with the same intensity and lack of attention (or tenderness?) I gave myself completely to my enemies. Before, before Joana.

So the waiter brought my Steinhaeger and another beer, and I ordered a small portion of salami. I made millions of conjectures and had a fundamental doubt and hope. Would Joana share my deepest, most miserable loneliness?

She assured me that she would. And she did more. She promised me a life with children, insignificances and meatballs. Great.

"Another shot, waiter."

I am not saying that it was enough, nothing like that. On the contrary, I have never been able to notice my shortcomings and this goddamn solitude (from which I fed, I should say) that made me bigger than I could ever be, the same solitude, by the way, that made me rejoice in myself and that, in the end (Damn it!) gave me all guarantees of blowing it all.

"Do you understand, waiter?"

It was a mixture of revenge and recognition. Regarding the grandiloquence and the menu served, as well as the lies, tricks and the dissimulated lack of interest of my genius. That son of a bitch.

The problem, once again, is that every now and then it was almost impossible to share the fruits of this foul mischance. Who would I share the mutiny with, after all?

With my fucking genius? Again?

"No, waiter, no fucking way."

Only Joana could go down with me. So, Joana, I have to say that this rejoicing has never been a contradiction or a total screw-up. Besides the guarantee of blowing it, I depended on the same pain and a feeling of demolition to move forward in the direction of the one I loved the most. The word "betrayal," therefore, is more appropriate than the expression "completely fake." It conveys an exchange, not necessarily a lie, but something closer, let's say, to an act of resistance, when it came to a solitary man like me. Before, before Joana.

Anyway, the results were in my favor, and I could discard beforehand any possibility of euphemism, and keep my stoic impulses under control.

"It's very simple, my friend. Bring me another beer."

I have always had all evidence, arguments and proofs of my grandeur. It couldn't have been any different. The reason, when I think about it, is that it gave me all the alibis and justifications for the deranged functioning of my goddamn genius. Hence, cheating, muttering catchphrases and hitting below the belt were my weapons, invariably lethal.

One fundamental piece of information: "I have never

come, waiter."

So, I could have left the stage quietly. "Like, fish farm-ing in Itatiaia," that was what I said to the waiter and repeated to the receptionist of Hotel Serrano after he confirmed the res-ervation Joana had made.

"That was all I really wanted—fish farming in Itatiaia! Oh, my good friend, Joana said yes!"

Take a look at that. Fish farming, salmon, maybe, or trout, to be a little simpler. Or better, Joana, me, the little In-dian, three other brats, duvets, dogs, cats, and if it weren't for all that I could never stand going back to writing. I didn't want to go back to writing.

I did, however. Here I am, writing a story that should not be written. When I came inside her, I wanted a daugh-ter, not another book. And Joana opened her legs and said yes, and I believed her and was fooled. But I couldn't think of going down the path of damnation again. If I had to do it, it would be against my will. Oh God, my God, why? I mean, before Joana I wrote to get revenge on life. I could never imag-ine—when I decided to let my guard down and take a chance on life—that Joana would do the dirty job for me. And she did more. She killed life and did so much more. She gave me a pregnant fiction in the place of my favorite little Indian. I don't know, maybe I shouldn't complain so much and maybe she has been too generous with me, and maybe she has given me back to myself, twofold. Ashes, undoings, death and destruc-tion, it was with these four elements that she fucked. I only contributed with love, which was too little, or almost nothing to her. Instead of a woman, I found an accomplice, and here we are. Here I am.

Murderer and murdered. Back and with doubled force, an even worse son-of-a-bitch. And now, (Why, God?) without any pain, without hesitating before annihilating those I loved the most and that loved me back, now I want to take double revenge on my fucked-up genius. It deserves it. I deserve it. I'm going to do it for the little Indian. And of course, it's me who will pay the price for managing (once more, until when?) to survive the curse.

"But who said I have exchanged life for art, waiter? No way, no fucking way. It's cheesy, but that's it. Bring me the bill and one for the road."

By the way, one thing that I find intriguing is the plea for more compassion on the part of those who love me. Why love? What for? There's no time for negotiation. I know what I'm saying. After writing the books I have written, I know. Fuck, it looks like no one understood me.

"If anyone wants my love, they'll have to share my murders," that was the second thing I said to the receptionist at Hotel Serrano. And he answered me, "I think it's a reasonable exchange. Your reservation is confirmed to June 18th, sir."

Another piece of information—when I talk about "murders," you have to give me some room and at the same time never hesitate. Love's grandiloquence and exaggeration, I would trade it all for a six pack of beer, drank against my will. Ah, before Joana things were rudimentary, tragic and predictable.

"Do you understand, waiter?"

JOANA LOVED ME MUCH MORE THAN I COULD HAVE IMAGINED

So much, that her absence is so powerful that not even her presence here and now would be enough to fill the void that devours me.

It is an emptiness which, before anything else, is a physical problem which only gets bigger and bigger, coming from a despicable, infernal equation established by Joana. "I love you. But I don't feel attracted to you." I know it is asking too much, especially after being kicked in the ass like I was, and I know it's beyond this girl's comprehension, but I would still like to ask, or wish, if it was possible, that she could love me the same way that I hate her in this very moment. This might be the first time I ask for something other than my hatred of someone. It doesn't matter that it's in vain, it doesn't matter that it is love. It doesn't matter, it doesn't matter. I need anything to put in the place of my soul, anything that can replace my rotting heart, which fills the emptiness that her absence left.

"If you love me, we can find this attraction together."

Isn't that simple? Unfortunately, it isn't. If I am making myself clear, after everything, I can no longer manage my own fall. I suffer for someone who doesn't want me, and she falls too.

There were times that I was really insufferable (I could always hold my own) and my only choice, facing my holocausts, was to ask too much. I never asked anyone to hate me less. The hatred I provoked was proportional to my talent, and commonplace was my fuel. It was simple, and that was the way it was. And I kept on going.

The situation was really unbearable. The difference was that, before Joana, the word "unbearable" did not exist for me. Whoever doesn't love—now I understand—aside from bargaining, can make use of paradoxes. And I was a pro at this. There. Before her, I was a perfect guy, and—although efficient—was almost impracticable. I used to go to barbecues, fuck whores and celebrate my birthday every year on May 9th. Everything was very simple. Sometimes—and this wasn't something rare—a Chicabon ice lolly can make a hell of a mess (of the sentimental kind). Sometimes—almost always— I solved the problem wishing magical, stumbling bananas and a procession of maidenhairs upon my enemies, and orchids. And everything moved softly on the parade of dead souls I had established to take to the ruins, both mine and others'. And there is more. I wished icy kisses on the faces of my torturers. And while I wasn't sincere, I could still find the time to lick the whores' pussies, set fire to beautiful houses on the beach with a sea view, and wish unconditional "Summers of '42" to Corinthians and Palmeiras rooters. Fuck them, and the entire world along with them.

Not now. Now it's different. I'm screwed. And I have a confession to make. I wanted to believe in God, one hundred percent. Everything would easily resolve, and I could be more gratuitous, more human. But I can't do it. All I have is Joana and my loneliness, and still it's not enough. Almost nothing compares to the love I feel for her.

It wasn't for the fuck we arranged

And it wasn't because we made—like two chimpanzees—the most beautiful plans of desire. Nothing of that sort. If everything went wrong, it was because, differently from what we had imagined (me, perhaps, more than her), we didn't manage, I didn't manage to free myself from the meanness and the demands of the morning after.

The pain, my pain, it comes from there.

We didn't need anything more than our intended love. If on our first meeting we arranged a quick fuck at Hotel Serrano, (she suggested the place, I had only suggested a neutral chamber) it was to escape all of that. At least I believed so.

I didn't need this book. Nor did she. Joana promised a life of insignificances and ornamental fish, although I insisted on the salmon, trips to Disneyworld and parent-teacher meetings, Sundays, television, queues.

"At midnight. The hotel is in Largo do Machado. On the 18th." Joana, wearing black panties in the emails, drunk on whiskey, mad to give it all to me. I was a little fatter than I was in the picture I'd sent her, and had a thick beard. She promised me Serzedelo Correa Square. Cod pastries in Santa Teresa.

"Of course, my love." She included clairvoyants, orchids, astral maps, her fucking foretelling skills to tell me yes one more time. She rented an apartment in Copacabana. I would be in charge of the picture frames and had to assemble the bookcase. I was going to close my small kitchenette in São Paulo and send Gadelha, my genius, to hell, before packing all my books and CDs and take everything to our apartment in Copacabana. After a cinematographic fuck, we would (together, Joana and I) organize her books with mine, combine our CD collections. I wanted to introduce Tony Lemos, the Elvis Presley of Apucarana, to Joana, not to mention I would brag about the balls, the purple earth and the places to the north of Ivaiporã I had never been to. Somehow, I was reinventing my repertoire for her, and I would add some stories about digging for gold in Canastra and the wreck of my ghost ship; everything to see her smile, to have her by my side.

Joana, 21 years old. One week before I had turned forty. I should not be here, today, at 4:21 am, looking at the Itaú clock from my kitchenette in Roosevelt Square. A goddamn emptiness. "Blue in Green," Miles Davis.

AH, MY LITTLE WOMAN

At this very moment, in Rio, that bitch must be sucking cocks in spirals. Afterwards, she will rest on some idiot's lap, instead of being here with me, listening to my lies. My little woman.

Yes, because she had said she was my little woman, and I was the older man from the cards. The foreteller, the clairvoyant, the astral maps and all that bullshit had all said so, and she had told me she would wait for me with black panties, smeared with lipstick.

What the hell happened, my love?

We didn't deserve that absence. I know how it hurts to sacrifice your life to write a book. When I say that, I am not being a proselytizer. And I know the level of lying that these sentences involve—literature is not made only of sperm, blood and soul. It's no good if a writer who bleeds, cums, lives and dies for this shit doesn't work hard to fuck his brains out, reason and do whatever is necessary to satisfy his own pain, an act of God, or whoever blames this broken son-of-a-bitch that was doomed to fly over abysses, write, write and get screwed, and become split in two, the two sides of the same coin. This is the beauty of it all. It's all I have, and it's nothing.

I bet, even though I knew in advance that I would

lose. I hit the wrong target deliberately, and got rid of the obligation of believing. Oh God, but I believe! It's not easy, especially in my case, to write in the first person and have the cynicism and the honesty of saying, "I have already been killed many times, and this was my last life."

For all those reasons, I didn't wear a condom. I bet everything I had inside of her, and I blew it. Desire killed love, that was what I understood, and I don't even care if I have got AIDS.

AND IT HURTS. IT HURTS TOO MUCH.

Everything started with an email. Joana had written a book and wanted me to take a look. In the message, she said I was her favorite writer. She asked for my address. "Is it possible?"
Then, I was the son-of-a-bitch I always was and decided to send her my address. I asked her for a "compromising" picture. The answer came with a little tight ass: "Hello, Marcelo. I sent you the book by post and my little ass by email. Kisses, Joana."
A prank. That could only be a prank. I invested in the game. It was my turn, now. I sent her a picture of me, wearing a tuxedo, on the beach, surrounded by beautiful girls and wrote, "Why don't you come with the book and bring the little ass?"
All in the same package—Joana, the little ass and the book. I was in Florianópolis (wearing a tuxedo), about ten kilos heavier and looking older, and she was in Rio de Janeiro, more beautiful, hotter, a radio and TV student, wearing a black thong, waiting for me.
"Marcelo, with a beard, fat and crazy to see me? I'm so happy I'll invest my thighs. Tomorrow, I'll be wearing some lipstick. Kisses, Joana."
I asked for more pictures and fell (did we fall?) into

the same trap. I made sure to fall, by the way. After that, Joana sent me pictures of her feet, her knees, her belly, one after the other. She sent me pictures of her tanned shoulders and of her nails, polished especially for me, of her bedroom, the little flower vase and "our apartment" where we would "fuck like crazy."

"I took a lot of pictures for you yesterday. Come soon! I'm happy. Kisses, Joana." For the first time, I realized that someone had "done something for me." I just didn't think about the question of who had taken the pictures.

I decided to set the date for our meeting for the 18th. I asked her for her phone number. She sent me an email on the following day. "Hello, Marcelo. I think I'll die of happiness. Today, I'm with a pregnant friend who came from São Paulo for a visit. She's going to spend a few days here. The 18th would be great because I'll be on holiday, with a new apartment, and wearing lipstick. I have all the pictures in the world for you. Take note of my number and call me."

A pregnant friend was something plausible. But the 18th seemed so far away. College holiday, a new apartment, lipstick and all the pictures in the world for me.

Now, after Joana had sent me pictures of almost all parts of her body, with the exception of her pussy, which she saved for the last photo before our meeting (displaying a "conservative cut"), she sent me a picture of her face, which I hadn't asked for. I didn't ask out of politeness, and because, at that point, it didn't matter to me. "This one goes to my favorite writer." Beautiful, twenty years old, a smiling brunette, with big teeth and a red mouth "waiting to kiss, kiss, kiss a lot".

It couldn't be a prank. I called her. She answered, calm and sweet, with a sleepy voice, made, let's say, to match the pictures, but didn't actually fit them (just like one picture didn't fit the other). She said she was shy, the daughter of a poet from Ceará and a mother who had killed herself at the age of 31. Joana had recently divorced a gringo, and read all of my books. I believed in, better yet, I was enchanted by her sleepy shyness, her hoarse voice and her soft carioca accent. Besides being her favorite writer, I was "the man of her life." During the phone calls that followed, we talked about dogs and cats, three sons and a daughter who would become my favorite child (the one Joana killed with the morning-after pill), details of domestic life, duvets, a small farm in Itatiaia, fish farming for me and high-tech horoscopes for her, families in São Paulo and Ceará, parakeets and parrots, and mainly (and strangely) amenities and silly things that had nothing to do with the kinky pictures and messages we exchanged via email. "I loved it when you called. Besides believing in horoscopes, I have big and well-shaped feet, almost like an L." She sent me another angle of her feet, this time with a cigarette lit between the toes. "Kisses from your Joana."

Oh. My Joana. My little woman. So she asked for my birth date and place. She would write my astral map and our synastry.

"What, Joana? Symmetry?"

(Here, Joana's several lovers must be feeling sympathetic towards me.)

This is called a collector's repertoire. But she didn't like the joke, and told me I should take the love she felt for me seriously. "Synastry, honey. The crossing of your astral map with mine."

Look at that. We have crossed our astral maps. This caused about a dozen hand jobs, one after the other. The curious thing is that, in spite of the jokes, I believed everything she said.

Sometimes I think she cast some kind of spell to involve me so completely. It's a shame that she decided to end everything herself. If it was up to me, I'd be her pet voodoo.

According to Joana, our synastry revealed the most

perfect balance. Kisses, kisses. "I can't wait for our time to come. Kisses, Joana."

She would wait for me wearing black panties. "I've also bought a dress to wear as I wait for you. I want to be very beautiful and very drunk when you arrive."

Desire was clear in the emails. The phone calls were sweeter and homier. I decided to give her an ultimatum. If she agreed, we'd live a perfect story, the kind that doesn't need to be written. So, I proposed a neutral ground for our first meeting on the 18th—A seedy hotel, at midnight.

Until that day, we wouldn't phone each other anymore. We would avoid emails and photos. Just our meeting, and not another word. I suggested that she wait for me drunk on wine. A new email arrived.

"Whiskey, my love. I'll be drunk on whiskey. What kind of hotel do you prefer? I was thinking of Serrano, which has a neon sign. It's in Largo do Machado. Not another word. I'm giving you my Valentine's Day gift in advance. Kisses, kisses, Joana."

Two round, rosy tits, a shaky picture. "Kisses, Joana, your little woman."

Aw, cute. A life without books, children and many kisses. And the cherry on top was that Joana had money and promised she would take care of everything, under the condition that I relaxed—forever.

São Paulo, in spite of myself

Of course she understood the message I left on her voice-mail perfectly. Now, she was the one who left three messages on mine, and none of them fit into the hypothesis I had started to put together during that night, before I decided to go back, when I woke up scared, and Joana wasn't by my side. I wished she had left me a message like "Rio de Janeiro is a beautiful city at dawn." The circumstances, however, just like my thesis, were much more tragic and perhaps weren't up to the love and vertigo I felt for that girl. Here's the situation: 1. Joana had realized her fantasy of fucking her favorite writer—me, the fool. 2. Bitch, whore, tramp, aroused...enchanted and beautiful.

The problem was that the desperate voice recorded on my voicemail told me the opposite: 1. She missed me. 2. She apologized for the misunderstanding (no double meanings involved here). 3. Fucking five times in a single night didn't mean anything, and no one has the obligation to provoke anyone's desire. 4. Her hypothesis, which I would refuse vehemently under any circumstance, was that she wanted to be my friend. 5. "She loved me." And 6, 7, 8, etc., etc. 9. "Don't ask me to explain." 10. "I feel very bad for not being your woman." And 11, 12...

Well, I did all I could. I reached for the phone and called Rio de Janeiro. I was practical and objective, like a morning-after pill.

"So, we're not fucking again?"

"I don't think so."

"You don't think so?"

"No, never again."

So things were more serious than they seemed. Or more confusing. And my love just became more impotent in face of the desire she didn't have for me. So much love, no desire at all.

And what about me? What was I going to do with the goddamn desire I felt for her? Shove it up my ass? So, we would never fuck again?

Nothing, no, never more?

Some beautiful things I remember

These were the things that came before the phone calls. I didn't know what had happened. I walked a lot during those days. Before the trip on the airplane. Before I saw Christ the Redeemer strangled among clouds of Bisurated Magnesia. I found a taxi which left me in Leblon. I invented farewells, included the suicidal mother and the half-obvious desire she had for her father. I also went into a shoe store in Catete and asked for the little Indian, in despair, and discovered a few things at a Macumba shrine. Here, however, this type of revelation doesn't matter to me. I want to talk about Joana, "in spite of myself."

She slept for almost twenty hours straight. If it was the effect of mixing the morning-after pill and antidepressants, and the ideas full of whiskey and lies that enchanted me so, then I could also talk about little sweet acts on Joana's part and irrelevancies she said, such as, "The pill gives me zits." And I also remember her concern about meeting me only after she was completely recovered, telling me not to call before. "I don't want you, I love you."

Our farewell was in Santa Clara, at ten o'clock at night. I was still staying at the seedy hotel in Catete. I arrived at eight.

Thursday—one day after Joana avoided me for the first time.

Friday, I met her at the Arabian restaurant. On that day, she actually dumped me. We cried a lot. A sweet, but tolerable situation. In that moment, we had made a beautiful goodbye scene.

Ten days before, we had dealt with that goddamn desire. From the little hotel in Largo do Machado ("Fuck me, you're the best writer in Brazil!"), we went to Lamas, and at five in the morning we walked around old Rio, and I couldn't hold her hand. Meanwhile, she chatted with her friend on her mobile phone. There was the kiss in the taxi. I walked a lot, cried even more.

Before, before the taxi. I walked with Joana until we reached Posto Três, and she held my arm like a pulp fiction heroine.

The most beautiful thing, however, was the ancient night which had already gotten rid of us both. We didn't notice at the time, but there was a beautiful full moon, if I recall correctly.

Joana assured me we wouldn't end everything like that. I don't even know why I rented that apartment in Leme. I don't know anything. The beach promised for the next day was nothing but a sweetness that had no chance of happening. I tried, I still try, to remember the best moments and I don't remember, I can't remember, her eyes.

The supernatural, Gilberto Gil, science, and all other tripe owe me an explanation. How could things have ended like that?

My hypotheses didn't make any sense. Oh God. I came inside her. Joana didn't object at all. We exchanged a cold beer kiss, and it was really good.

I was also happy to share "something" with another person. We had killed the little Indian together. Did that make me happy? Yes, yes, very happy, because for the first time I wasn't alone and had an accomplice.

Joana & I, from that moment on, would live a life of little things. All I wanted for "the both of us" was to meet Zagallo jogging along Copacabana beach. That was it. Double parking and the Botafogo shopping mall. I was going to start working out, and buy some sports clothes. Of course, everything was already set. I had the formula, and my job as a rebel writer. Money wouldn't be a problem. Besides, I could give workshops, organize literary events and become Bonassi's partner. I would never write a real book again. I was going to sell myself shamelessly. If the occasion called for it, I could write some soap operas for Globo TV with Fernanda Young as my tutor. I wanted Joana to be proud of me. I wanted her to spend all my money. But what the hell happened?

Why São Paulo? Now, at four in the morning? I will repeat, I came inside her. I was going to move to Rio de Janeiro. She said yes, I'm sure. We cried. We lived a love affair as if I were Vinicius de Moraes and she was Hilda Hilst—the forty-something and the little woman. Wasn't that what happened?

Of course it was.

Or perhaps someone who knew voodoo had sewn my picture to a toad's mouth and buried it in Vicente Celestino's tomb. It's ten past four in the morning and I can't sleep. Her name is Joana. I should say that the woman who took my heart is called Natércia, but I won't do that, because I'm weak and I'm still in love, in spite of myself, in spite of the Frenchman with the red wine name that she met the following week. I won't say that she's called Natércia because she was honest with me. After dumping me, she made a collect call to my house and told me she "loved me," that she was "going out" with the idiot Frenchman, and that, if it was up to her (and not to the goddamn desire), she would leave the *forestier* and die by my side.

The problem was the goddamn desire. The problem was having to hear those aberrations during a collect call, because it was me *who loved her*. I can't understand what happened, honestly. But I can talk about it. I have the authority to do so.

Since this is the criteria, I mean, suffering like a chimpanzee and hearing myself in all the FM station songs, from Zezé di Camargo & Luciano's country music and Nando Reis' sappy ballads to Caetano Veloso and Morris Albert, well, if Joana loves me and it's going to rhyme anyway, I can say I know what it's all about. "I confess that I have lived," like Pablo Neruda, Adelaide Carraro and everyone else who affirms the same thing: "I love you."

Well, after having committed an "I love you" for the first time in my life, it was difficult to go back to Primo Levi, almost impossible to reread Cioran. After having practiced the amorous conscience of foolishness, a man effectively becomes an idiot, goes down into the gutter and stays there.

* * *

Last night I dreamt of Joana laughing in my face. She was fucking the Frenchman with the red wine name and, a beautiful whore, avoided the French kisses at the same time that she gave him the best head in the world, as if she were a professional. This was the same woman that had promised me a life with cable TV and children studying at the elementary school close to home, the same woman who I had lost because desire had killed love. If I was her, I would have charged him for the service.

That's it. What follows is a sappiness which will finally turn into revenge, hatred and disillusionment. I don't want dramatic boleros, no Lupicínio, no Vinicius de Moraes.

No, I don't want that. I don't have the patience or the greatness for that. And she doesn't deserve it.

What's left for me, here in the gutter, is part of my memory. I will, therefore, quote an excerpt of "Seven Nights." Jorge Luis Borges, who talked about "alephs" because he'd never eaten pussy, discussed Schopenhauer and Buddha. Both Siddhartha (or Buddha, it's the same) and the somber philosopher believed that the world was a dream and it would be very good if we stopped dreaming it every now and then. Buddha had a question, "What is to live?" If we simplified the whole thing, which is already redundant in this case, we would arrive at more or less the same terms Buddha did himself, "To live is to be born, to get old, to get sick and to die." Nevertheless, he believed there was more to it. One day, we would abandon our marble kitchenettes (Siddhartha abandoned his) and would have to suffer with other ailments, including one that Buddha himself believed to be the most pathetic, not being with those we love. Bull's eye.

A pair of dice. Three thousand years ago, Amado Batista lived his second incarnation, as an invertebrate curiously similar to the lyrics of his songs today. There, we have a good theme for debate between Creationists and Darwinists. I'd rather stay out of it. Joana is enough for me.

But there's no doubt that Buddha's wisdom is a perfect musical counterpoint to Amado Batista's lyrics. There's no obvious yin/ yang, no paradox, no Borges that will convince me of the opposite. Well, as I was saying, either the chap drinks himself to a stupor or he enters a monastery. He could also do what I've done- drink himself to a stupor, write a book and beg her to come back, even though he knows the girl is a tramp and will certainly cheat on him while she laughs in his Buddha's illuminated face, even though he knows that she has no desire for him and that he is an incorrigible ass who cries with Caetano Veloso singing "Feelings." Oh, Joana, I love you so much.

All I wanted was to get her pregnant. I would honestly give away all my books to be able to follow Joana's dark belly growing. Joana, who loved me for one night only. The result is that sometimes I dream of a little girl. She has my eyes, sad and round. She is Ritinha (or the Little Indian), my daughter. In the dream, Joana and I have decided that the little Indian's look is the same as mine. So, it's the look, not the eyes. A sad look that asks, with every new dream, to be born again. The little girl wants her mother. Joana disappears. The little girl and I don't know what to do. We have only the same sad look in our eyes.

It's not that the little girl was lost in my dreams. The morning-after pill would never have this power. However, the little girl becomes sadder and sadder, and looks more and more like me. It's as if the little girl and I were dreaming together, the same dream, the same desolation, the same lozenges of Ilha Porchat of my childhood, and a grey beach in winter.

I'll tell you something. I had thought that by being honest with myself, not avoiding writing what I wanted, I don't know, I would get rid of myself, be happy, and still have the little Indian.

But things were just not like that. I have never been so tormented, and what is worse, I lost the enchantment of my suicidal times. I missed the right target. I can't even aim for the right target anymore. There was a time when it was all or nothing. Now, I don't have that. I used to choose sacrifice, and be reborn. Now, I can't.

Oh, my daughter. I tried.

If I told you that it was difficult to get here and that I

didn't know what to do in the airport, and that I've used the money I earned writing about other people's little things to walk around like a zombie looking for you, ah, if I told you that I've tried to find you in the wombs of honest whores, and that you were never more than a dream of mine, ah, if I told you a lot of things, I would still be only "dreaming of you" again. I don't want that. Not for you, nor for me.

The only thing that has made me happy along this path, I'm sorry, my daughter, but I'll have to repeat it, was eating a heart of palm pie at the Galeão airport. Ah, my darling.

I cast off my demons and sent transcendence to hell. If I had repeated everything my bad conscience and the damn flow wanted to tell me, if I had trusted myself blindly, I swear, we would have met.

What if I told you that I did exactly that? And that I lost you, and that it served for nothing? I don't even know if we dreamed the same dream.

What could I have done? I returned to São Paulo. I'm a sad, lonely guy at five in the morning. That's what the Itaú clock on Paulista Avenue tells me. What about you, little Indian, where are you?

I have decided that in a few moments, at dawn, I'll have my Father's Day. You know, my dear daughter, it would be very easy to say I fell in love (again) with the wrong woman and that she, Joana, had nothing to do with the mother you were looking for. But I won't insist on this point. If I insisted again, I would be making the same mistake as always. I'd be only setting the record straight. My record. Enough!

I don't want to set the record straight anymore. I know more or less who I am, and I know that you exist and depend on me, somewhere. Yes, we dream the same dream. And there's more. Our uncrossed paths are the same. Here, looking at the clock that tells me it's 5:50 a.m., as it is there in Largo do Machado where you were conceived, or in Copacabana, where your mother sleeps despite the full moon and the abortions she has made. It doesn't matter, my darling, I just want to say that the circumstances do not matter, or better, they are nothing but evidence that you and I, my little Indian, arrived, again, to the wrong place.

The absence

It is dawn. Joana's absence is stronger than my abandonment. It's such a shame that she doesn't know about the intensity of the pain she caused me. If she knew, maybe she could be healed of herself and come back, and erase this absence that is bigger than her. I have to say, the pain starts to block the esophagus, and it spreads like grease from the inside, extending out of the body and reaching the streets and all public places, making this guy (because I'm not myself anymore) write old song lyrics, cross the road without looking and stumble over the emptiness, facing a self which spins around nothing and its widespread undoings. Ah, if Joana knew about the mutilation, and the evil, and how much I miss her, maybe she would even feel guilty and recognize that she's a (beautiful, beautiful) whore and maybe she would become aware of her own cruelty, of the manipulation that can only return to her, the mistress of a damned merry-go-round of undoings. Ah, if she knew how much I miss her, she would consider this "information" a survival guide, and from there, she would have no choice but to do what I'm doing now. As the sun rises, I suffer for the love she denied herself and me. And yet she will never know how much I miss her. There is a physical absence, which occupies my respiratory system and the greyest expressways of the city, a void that brings places closer to me, makes them smaller and turns them all into the same thing—an absence that makes this guy cry on the underground train, and is the cause of his limp dick, that has no explanation and that surprises his beloved on the other side of the platform, only to lose her the next minute. An absence that makes him (the poor guy) shrink in his aloofness, takes him hostage in the most detestable commonplaces at dawn, every dawn he spends without her. Ah, if Joana arrived here and now, at this exact minute, I repeat, her presence wouldn't be stronger than this emptiness that devours me. It would be nothing compared to the flabbiness that occupies all spaces, aortas, squares, carotids and supermarkets that ceased to exist in her absence. I think she could throw baby showers for her whore friends and suck the cocks of all transvestites in Lapa. She could make fun of her own lunacy and fly merrily over murders. She could drive a European tourist, a centenary tree, an income tax officer, a swan or a Pataxó Indian mad with desire, and she could fuck them all and be raped by them all at the same time. But nothing would fill her with the absence that brings me down and makes all my curses useless, an impossible prayer that begs her to come back. She could have as many abortions as she pleases, and try to avenge her mother's suicide on the walls of her own womb, and be pierced by the emptiness of solitude, and suck her father's cock, the same way she tries to avoid kisses (as if she were a hangover black hole), but she will never, ever, suffer from the absence I feel, not even if she gets dumped the same way she dumped me. She will never feel this absence, so intense and so deep inside the chest. She will never know how much I miss her, nothing, never.

Only I can feel the weight of this absence and know the price I pay for being here, writing this goddamn book against my will. It's not only a case of listing my other disgraces and reiterating my indignation, but also a case of talking about the money I lose for not doing anything better than this. This is redundant, at least in my case. I no longer believe the "artifice" which, in theory, and as "fiction"—as if it was literature, art, or all those silly things made by those who can't see an inch beyond their noses—is only good to fuel other people's delight. I'm more selfish than eternity, and I quit, I retire from the idealized and living worlds. I'm screwed. I'm not the type of person who clarifies things, either. I'm sorry for those who don't understand me. I'm screwed, period.

Should I feel sorry for myself, too? Or consider myself lucky because now, after losing Joana and throwing away the best I had, I didn't get anywhere?

I don't know. There's only one thing I know—the absence is stronger.

And this personal failure makes me focus, somehow, on things that matter only to me, and it has brought me to this non-place called Joana, a place that is larger than my understanding. The absence is the only thing I "practice," the only thing that remained of the debris called literature, from which I feed, and which poisons me. And then there's freedom...

I can't forget about the damned freedom. It was for this freedom that I annihilated all my chances of being happy. It was for freedom (and later, for the absence) that I got old before my time, and it was because of this shitty freedom that I got here, deeply upset, writing another great book that doesn't have anything to do with me. So, the losses are countless, and because of the freedom acquired, and all "facts that contain the curse," I evidently had to have my counterpart—pride. Yes, pride and vanity. Pride in being able to write my own death certificate and in understanding the greatness of the curse and somehow using it as an instrument of repulsion and combat, killing and being killed. Or better, if I don't have another choice, or if I have to be screwed and be used by all commonplaces, at least I can stand up and yell, "Muses instincts, God, the fucking devil and everything else" I will be broken in pieces and change life into art, but I couldn't care less about this art. I would happily trade my genius for the little Indian, to see her eating a Chicabon ice lolly. Even with the regrets and the wrong choices, I wouldn't hesitate for a minute before making this choice, and you can write that down.

And there's another thing. I have learned to recognize the weapons Joana used to love me and to destroy me, but this doesn't mean that I have understood her or that I'm cured of the kick in the ass. No way.

Joana stabbed me deeply and did a good job. She wiped me off the map. This is one of her qualities. But there's something to be said here—I only admit to being wiped off the map once. The fact that I have asked her to come back doesn't mean I have capitulated, only that I still love her, and I think that I'm another person now. Besides, she wouldn't do any half-injustices. Joana isn't the kind who gives in. She isn't the kind that will walk in my shoes—first of all, because she's selfish, and second because that's my place, not hers; beautiful, enchanted cocksucker. I don't want to believe it, but if she comes back, I'll regret it.

I think she'll just get screwed by me. Only I know how shattered I was to confront what is rightfully mine, compared with what I have become—a lonely, bitter man, and unfortunately (I never learn...), a believer in the fury and the love of my executioners. It's eight o'clock in the morning and I haven't slept. I don't have Joana. I'm a sadist when I should be a masochist, and a masochist when I should be a sadist.

I don't want to demand greatness from anyone, it's not that. The problem lies in managing the feeling of smallness. I won't admit that feeling. No fucking way! Despite the tragedy of enjoying freedom, I have I have a hell of a lot of pride, and an obstinate reason for claiming calamity in the same proportion as surrender—a shared sacrifice. So I ask Joana to give me another chance, to come back, but do not spare me. I won't be compassionate, because love is the worst counselor. I'll love Joana until the end. I will love her as someone who loves their executioner and as someone who stabs their worst enemy, as if I were "doing the job" for her, until the end.

I'll repeat it a thousand times—this is the price I pay for being here, writing this book. It is my own foul mischance. There isn't a term to define it, nor a measure for the sacrifice. And in spite of how much I miss her, the only possible premise, the only place to start changing things lies with me, and no one else. Not even Joana, could change this, turn it back. This is my obligation.

It doesn't help to dissimulate, to find excuses, let's say, to get to hate from love. It also doesn't help to elect affinities to avoid confrontation. I was wiped off of Joana's map and all I can do is scream about everything I miss (and that died before existing).

Therefore, this is no attempt to redeem myself, me projecting the image of a little girl with the same sad, blurred look in her eyes, a little girl who doesn't exist. This is only another symptom of your absence, Joana, here and now, when I imagine your beautiful, sad eyes which are actually my eyes, and the little girl's eyes that look at impossible wonders, dead and killed before existing. So, Joana, from one bout of crying to another, I try but I can't refuse the miracle as if it were a curse, as if we weren't exactly the same despicable people, one murdering the other, one dissolving into the other, fucking through the night as two chimpanzees that contradict each other and shut themselves down. So, this love will never be any good. And maybe you're right, our over-abundant love will both never be enough, and at the same time, will be stronger.

I have to agree with this, I am forced to agree. The difference is that you will never understand the dimension of the worm and the prerogatives of the giant that compromise you, and your pride, with which is very easy to "execute" the intention of a successful abortion, it will only pay a sterile tribute to the germ. So, you'll be suffocated by greatness, and your curse will be carried out and interrupted halfway. But I know the exact measure of my greatness and I know exactly what I am and the price I pay for being here—writing this book against my will, demanding from you the fruit you will never give me because you exist only to fill me with absence, to be my other half, the half of me the day after, dead.

I decided that I wouldn't be the plush vampire of a girl who wouldn't give in to me. Oh, what foolishness. It is obvious that, not because of Joana, but it was due to my own latent, alive vampirism at her disposal.

Joana called me in the middle of the night, crying. She said she had a fever. She was sick and was participating in the filming of a movie. On the other end of the line, I could hear little screams, the noises from a sad party, and a slow moaning. She also told me I shouldn't have abandoned her, I shouldn't have "left." She said she would kill herself. She said things like "Come back, my love," and "forever is no more." There was a tragic, enchanting feeling in her phone calls. A death strategy. An addiction.

The whole night, I would hang up and she would call again, crazier and more desolate. So I felt sad for her. Sad, because, besides having internalized Joana's private tragedies, the things she said by not saying anything, such as the story about the Frenchman with the red wine name, sounded like fun, and Joana (I kept telling myself) would call me to calm herself down a little, to think about something other than the film party, and also to enjoy, once again, the thought of having dumped me. "I feel so bad for not being your woman."

Actually, Joana was a strong woman, full of fucking premeditation, enchanting and lethal, and maybe she didn't know that. If she did know, then she didn't have full control over that enchantment. Go figure. Often, during those phone calls, I would hear a voice asking for her, calling her in the middle of clouds of vapor, and giving orders, "Drink, Joana. We'll talk to the dead woman later and see what she thinks." She didn't obey the voice, however, or she answered the calls slowly and vaguely, at the same time she cried on the phone and told me she felt very lonely, actually, that she loved me. Maybe Joana had a vague suspicion about the bridge she was building over the stupid abyss she was flying above, and the absence that I suffered with. I still don't know. What I still carry with me is an urgency that lasts late into the nights, an effective absence. A lack of understanding.

So I became sad because I always fell into the traps she set for herself. Joana and I worked in synchronicity. We used the same methods and I could finally point to infinite coincidences that would only increase my anguish and perplexity with her abandonment. But I don't want that. The slow nights and her absence are enough for me. I can't do anything for myself or for her anymore.

On the other end of the line is a Rio de Janeiro of sad parties and slow moaning, almost paralyzed. Here, in São Paulo, there are only endless nights...

It was as if I had to suffer the vertigo of reality and refused to believe in the novelty of an encounter gone wrong. It was a delicate situation to begin with, because I suffered from an incomplete vertigo, with bumps and zigzags, and then because I suffered the pain of paths uncrossed, from the blockage of my esophagus to the pain in my stomach. I had to deal with my idealization and with a full blockage that became undone, only to return because of the nightmares, the suffocation and Joana's phone calls throughout the night.

I dreamt of Joana, and, in the middle of the night, while we were on the phone, she wanted to know the color of the dress she wore in my dreams. I couldn't tell. I only knew that the *dream* was red. Joana floated over a red platform, and was happy. That was what happened in my dreams, and again during the phone calls. What really bothered me was waking up and remembering her instead of feeling thirsty, running to the bathroom to pee, or any of those normalcies that occur when we wake up in the middle of the night, no matter if awakened by a nightmare or a phone call. I want to say one thing, were it a dream, I would have dreamt it. The problem was that it was actually a phone call from a sad party in Rio de Janeiro and I had Joana on the other end of the line. The best moments became the worst memories. She's still with me today, and I miss her, I miss her very much. I don't think even the idealization of a love affair, not even the repetition of the first email, "here goes my little ass," or each step leading to the kick in the ass in the Arabian restaurant would be enough. Not even if she arrived, and she will never arrive, I repeat (again, again), would her presence be larger than her absence. It is not a case, then, of saying that I've lost her, but the opposite! I have Joana, begging me, "Don't ask me why. I love you."

Nothing could, or will, fill the absence. Not even emptiness. Not even if a whole zoo of chimpanzees decided to fuck on my behalf. Nothing will fill the absence, or compensate for the explanations and lack of explanations. Nothing has any importance anymore, because she's here by my side, now more than ever.

She didn't leave me. I would say that Joana is more than my heteronym. She exists because she's simultaneously my cheating double and absence itself.

Closer and closer and against her will.

The ass-kicking, the spiral kisses she tried to avoid, Christ the Redeemer strangled by clouds of Bysmuth Magnesia. Slow moaning, the sad party, she never left, and everything was Joana and the late nights...

"I feel love for you. Isn't that enough?"

"What time is it, Joana?"

"I love you."

"I love you, too."

"Then, why...?"

"Don't ask any questions, my love."

"Never again?"

"No, never."

"It's twenty to four. Your dress was red in my dream. I think it was red."

"I knew I could count on you."

"I want to fuck you again..."

"Don't talk like this."

"Why not?"

"This is all shit. The director is a crazy dyke."

"It's probably your fault."

"She asked me for a kiss the other day."

"So?"

"It was good, but that was it."

"I know, I know. I think I should have spanked you. You wanted to be spanked, didn't you?"

"What?"

"You wanted to be spanked. You wanted the demented man from the books...the guy who burns women's asses with cigarette butts and leaves the morning after without paying the hotel bill. And when I showed up, caring and loving, sucking your little tits and wanting nothing more than the missionary position, you decided to dump me. That was it, wasn't it?"

"It was beautiful, the way you loved me."

"What happened?"

"I have to go back to shooting. We'll talk later. I love you."

A few conjectures. I was planning a reunion. I wanted to look into her eyes again, to set the record straight. If on one hand, and according to her craziness, I had to respect the desire she *didn't* feel for me, on the other, and following the same logic, she would also have to respect the desire I felt for her. An honest vice-versa is the least I could demand from that lunatic who called me in the middle of the night to tell me she loved me and would never fuck me again.

My soul for Joana's sex, or no deal. I tried to be cynical when I made the proposal, acting like a total jerk so she would give everything up and so we could, from the color established by my, our, dreams —red, finally end the love we felt for each other. She accepted.

But it could never work. Not in practice. It was impossible in every way. If she wanted me as her plush vampire, if she wanted to be "my friend," she shouldn't be anywhere near me, because my suffering would make her desire turn into something else. I couldn't care less. I didn't mind if it turned into hatred, frustration, desire for a dyke or for a framed photograph. I didn't care that she didn't want to fuck me, but loved me. She'd be better off loving the Dalai Lama.

Friendship should be friendship. I have my friends, and they're my friends and I will tell you why: we don't have sex. I wanted to make things more difficult for her. I was that pretentious. According to my calculations, soon Joana would offer me her sex, and ask for my soul in return. On that day, I would be a total jerk. I would be crueler to her than she had been to me. Meaning, I would use her and then leave her, telling her we could never do that again because, after all, *we loved each other.* And that was nothing compared to the love I feel, or felt, for her, and the desire that she didn't feel for me. Goddamn desire. Goddamn love.

I wanted to be tough with Joana on the phone. I made conjectures, organized my thoughts, and planned an improbable attack on her because I had been dumped and she would never change her mind. It could only end in nothing. If I had managed to keep a solemn tone, it was only until she started to cry on the phone. I couldn't help myself and cried with her. It was actually very beautiful. The intriguing thing is that I started to have an erection. I told her that.

"I think I'll jerk off for you, my love."

Fuck the desire that she didn't have for me. I had enough for both of us. And I had lost all my arguments and my engineering failed anyway. I came, releasing some thick spunk, and asked her if that wasn't what she really wanted.

"Do you think this hot spunk isn't yours, Joana?"

She wept and smiled on the other end of the line. The tense atmosphere of the end of an affair and tragic separation became some sort of castrated seduction game. Joana wanted to listen to Roberto Carlos with me. Of course. I could order breakfast for two. And thinking about breakfast in bed, I jerked off in circles again for her. Everything about Joana went like this.

"The desire can be invented," I assured her. She told me to stop the nonsense and started to cry again. She told me about the fight she'd had with her sister and the movie she was shooting. The result wasn't pleasing to her, and she would have to wake up early the next morning to go to class. She had sniffed a lot of cocaine the night before, and had started a "too obvious affair" with her film professor.

"Don't talk to me about your affairs."

"Not even the obvious ones?"

"Especially the obvious ones, Joana."

She was having fun on the other side of the line and promised to limit the conversation to her father.

"All right. If it's with your father, you can talk about it."

It was all right, really. The situation was too obvious and, worst case scenario, would give me arguments to crush

Joana, and I needed that. After all, she felt bad for depending on her greatest love, her father, for survival. It does not get more obvious than that.

What I call my total lack of a talent for cruelty, in addition to Joana's soft skin and the memory of her wet pussy, drove me crazy. I wanted to be fooled. I would do anything, even encourage her love for her father, to have her by my side, confident and crushed, as if that was possible...

But Joana only confirmed her cruelty and checked another item off her list, being the enchanting whore that she was. She asked me to lend her a thousand reais.

"I'll deposit the money tomorrow, my love."

Ah, desire. I'd never thought playing the fool would give me such pleasure.

"But I'll pay you back, ok?"

Bingo!

"Don't worry..."

"I'm feeling sad, lonely."

"Me too, Joana."

"Would you stay with me forever?"

"Forever, my love."

Hell.

I WOULD LIKE TO CLOSE THE SUBJECT WITH JOANA'S CRAZY MOVES, LITTLE GAMES AND ZIGZAGS

It would be best to forget her lunacy and let it all go. Forget her. But I can't. When it comes to Joana, forgetting isn't possible.

Or better, this matter can't be closed so quickly. That's another problem. I think that behind all the lunacy, there is some unsuspected evil, something that comes from earlier times, a kind of reason to explain the whore that she is— someone with a strong tendency for manipulation and cruelty. Joana, in my guess, wants revenge because of her suicidal mother and a death by suicide (I'm talking about emptiness and not the act itself) in which she is regarded in a diabolical way. It is from there that the biggest paradox comes. The same movement that buries her resuscitates her from that mess. And there is more—the fuel that feeds these comings and goings is the mother's suicidal (and improbable) sex, meaning her strength is also her abandonment...as though cruelty could be both amorous and generous.

I'll try to explain. A bout of crying, which lasts for about five minutes, could erase from her memory all the fucking and all the abortions had the morning after, as well as wakes her up for an unlikely "slice of *pepperoni*, waiter, and two beers," Suddenly, it was as if taking the morning-after pill meant just another round of ice cold beer coupled with the next day's hangover. I was evidently dead already, sad and charming, wandering around a Rio de Janeiro that no longer exists. Under these circumstances, I have to admit that Joana is unbeatable, beautiful, and extremely fun. She knows how to get rid of other people and her own sex as if they were portions of fried cheese, little chicken hearts, bar food. The problem is that Joana is forced to eat the food and repeat the order (or commit suicide, whichever) several times. And she can't count on herself or the nice waiter, and can count even less on her mother, who killed herself (or avenged herself) only once. All Joana has left are methods and choices, sometimes terminal, sometimes enchanting, but only if her body can hold the incredible weight of her soul, which flowers sadly in the devil's pastures.

"Her bottom teeth are crooked, how sweet."

So, Joana isn't only a collector of males and females. This category presupposes the superposition of layer over layer of dead meat and, of course, a competent butcher to assemble one soul on top of the other, to "organize everything." And it's exactly there that Joana gets screwed again. She is included in the meat, so she collects herself too. That is, based on a loving detachment, Joana gives shamelessly to her enemies (or occasional lovers, either way) what is left of her humanity and plays her tricks as a manipulative female, an improbable, incendiary mix, a trap into which I fell and would still fall anywhere and anytime, like a stupid duck. I love that woman.

To use another cliché, I would say that she's the daughter of vertigo, and no one fits into the abyss she has created for herself. I suspect that only my own abyss could save me from Joana's. What I need is my own fall. What I have is her absence.

This afternoon, for example, I called Joana's house at

the same time that her cell phone rang. I overheard part of the conversation. She was telling someone named Kako to call her back in five minutes, and sent him a kiss. The same hoarse, sleepy kiss she would send me a moment later.

I felt sorry for this Kako, but I understood I was being foolish. No one, no fool in this world, would give himself away to Joana's vertigo and fall like I did. No one would believe her like I did, and no one would feel her absence as I still do today, after all the evidences of tragedy, after being ass-kicked and mainly after the money I deposited into her account. No one could be so stupid and infatuated as I was, am, and always will be.

"Forever?"

"Yes, my love, forever."

* * *

She still calls me, after everything, and tells me that the Frenchman with the red wine name vanished and then reappeared, and that he's quite a good fuck (but if it was up to her, she would gladly trade him for me). She complains about the obsession she simultaneously developed from her suicidal mother and her "all too obvious death." She says she's calling because she got a new sofa and that she isn't the bitch I know she is. She lights a cigarette on the other end of the line (the same cigarette that brings her relief and makes her a supposedly different girl), and I am perplexed with desire. She says that the Frenchman isn't important, that she's alone, that she feels no attraction to me, and I tell her again that we can invent it, we can find the damn desire somewhere. She doesn't want me. She knows I wake up in the middle of the night, shaking and scared, and that I cry because of her. So she plays dirty, and says she's coming to visit me if I pay for the plane ticket and deposit one thousand reais into her account again.

I tell her she kisses like a whore and she agrees, and she does more, she says it was her father who taught her to kiss like that, and asks me what my relationship with death is, and I want to know if she's talking about a death suffered, mine, or a death provoked, someone else's. And I tell her I died when she promised a life of children and meatballs. She changes the subject, because she knows this is a stupid idealization on my part, and that there is another game to be played. But she denies the game and betrays herself, for a fleeting instant, and that's why I have survived and why I'm here, or at least I think so. When she says she *doesn't love me*, and then she tells me about the visit from two friends that broke the windows of her new apartment, and that she misses her mother, then I, on the other end of the line, tell her that I've lost twelve pounds and that I have never, after our fuck, been able to get a hard-on for another woman. The confusion changes the pace of Joana's breath, makes her switch into second gear and forget about her mother, and it also makes me remember the sad look in the eyes of my unborn little Indian, and then I have the conviction that there was some serious lack of violence on my part, that I should have slapped Joana hard and burned her with the same cigarette butts from my books, and she says no. She seems to be reading my thoughts, and reaffirms that there was never any desire, and asks me to stop insisting on the subject, because it's the third time I insist, asking, "How is that? What about the five times we fucked that night?" She says, "For the last time," that the night in question had absolutely no importance and that she loves me. I don't make any further comments because I know Joana has just betrayed herself again (I want it to be so). So the conversation goes around the same axis (not necessarily an unstable one) and she lights another cigarette, and I insist once more and I can't understand and I know she is telling me the truth and I know she's lying and I decide to deposit the money into her account.

I love Joana.

* * *

Her gold-digging is so obvious, and, to make things easier, I open my doors to her with such eagerness that sometimes, due to the blindness I forced upon myself, I believe in Joana's moods completely. I believe her and she returns to my open door, asking and giving and acting as if she were a distracted whore, or as if she wasn't gaining and/or planning to gain some advantage that would evidently end up destroying her. The thing is, we have fooled ourselves (I'll break into pieces for love). And after so much time and despite everything, we managed to keep the chimpanzee night untouched, holding no grudge.

Holding no grudge! Where hatred should be, there is a feeling of mutual tenderness. The use of the soul is indeed an obscenity, and in this sick exchange, where we trade the flesh for the soul, we are professional actors, stray dogs. She dodges a French kiss like a whore, but she is not a whore, because she flees in spirals. I believe in spirals! I believed, as if the kiss was possible, or as if, at this point, it was possible for me to be only a fool. What hurts the most is the fair game, on both sides. I think that's it.

IT IS OBVIOUS I AM NOT THE SAME MAN AS BEFORE

She changed me. To get rid of this "before," I had bet all my golden chips on Joana...it was my only way out. Maybe I was a bad gambler. Maybe it wasn't even a competition once I started betting all my chips in the wrong place. Maybe I haven't changed. Since the very beginning I've tried, in the most violent and demented ways, to find love. Maybe what happened was that I uselessly distracted the audience, and myself. I had Joana's love in such an intense, corrosive way that not even in my wildest dreams could I have imagined the consequences. Regardless of whether I have changed or not, it doesn't matter.

The sure thing is that I have lost her. And now it won't do me any good to complain about the loss, or to beg for her love again. That would be the same as having hope in something that was consummated in itself, and that dragged me along with it.

I can say that I will never understand what happened, and that I feel perplexity and emptiness, and have frustrated expectations and a cry for help recorded in my voicemail. I have only one day after another without Joana, and a stupid wish to forget all of this. Now, I'm a lonely guy who accumulates losses. Before her, I had only my loneliness. Before her, although it might sound untrue, I understood myself.

Indifference and distance brought about by time, the indifference and distance that she acquired the same instant she dumped me, promised me a future in which, let's say, Joana would be my witness, as if I had a date with myself to kill or be killed, and what is worse, as if I had to commit suicide instead of Joana. At least this was what I understood from the last message she left in my voicemail.

I DEFEND THE FREEFALL

I'm almost like a cardinal of the late Pope John Paul II. I don't believe in condoms. All safe sex is a truism that might lead to death. Love, only love, and not "preservation" and its derivatives, can serve as a parameter for the time of suffering. And only if we take into account that hatred is born from love and that the human species has a chronic lack of compassion, madness and a good microwave oven to watch the butter popcorn bags swell. Besides, I defend the death penalty for whoever invented chicken pastries and honestly wish that Ed Motta would never sing "Beatriz," the most beautiful song in all of Brazilian popular music, again, because he destroyed it. I want to ask God's forgiveness, and I want to ask Him to punish my enemies severely before forgiving them. I would also like to win a DVD and a beautiful trip to Ituporanga, the land of the onions, and have the love of a waitress named Marilise as a bonus, as well as the autumn sun and memories. Am I asking too much? From the time I was just a boy and the lozenges of Ilha Porchat Club made me feel numb, I had the perspective of a bottle of Pepsi-Cola, a half-psychedelic, half-sad thing that I have never, despite the Brazil Channel on cable TV, had the chance to feel again due to my scepticism and my inability to fly, something I acquired with time, after everything, after Joana.

And there's another thing. Now that I'm back in São Paulo, I ask myself, "What could Rio de Janeiro have done for me, without her? Why was I so lonely in that city, after loving Joana, and why didn't I have another spark of the desire that I had saved for a lifetime, and would only led me to that encounter? What was it for, anyway?"

Was I looking for a sterile, tasteless astonishment, a mix of recognition and perplexity, triple chins and the immobility so similar to the apartment blocks of Barata Ribeiro in Copacabana?

Was that it?

Is there no space to fall into? What the hell happened to me? Have I become a fallen statue made of grease? A mixture of everything that was denied to me, of everything I got just because I took hold of it?

I don't want, besides sharing the murders, to share also the "bitterness or the truth" with my opponents here. They don't deserve the contempt I feel for myself. They are lesser people. I repeat, I wish sheer unhappiness to the women that didn't want me. To the others, who were paid in advance, I wish successful businesses and a Happy New Year.

To Joana, a woman who wanted me, the only thing I can say is that I'll love her forever, in spite of myself and in spite of her, even if it's too late.

Rio de Janeiro, São Paulo

I think about the lie (?) that Joana told me, and that, despite everything, it's still convincing today. And I don't understand how she, before getting into the taxi, managed to give that hug after our chimpanzee night as if it were the most beautiful, or the last hug we would engage in. And she didn't tell me anything. And I can't understand, either, why I'm here alone, looking at the Cantareira mountain range from my kitchenette, feeling sorry for the love I lost (or the aborted daughter). And then I remember all the comings and goings that are in fact a lie. But it can't be a lie because it hurts. Then I think about my fireworks. My fireworks aren't meant for other people to rejoice in. They should merely be fireworks, as if they were lies—like they used to be, when I used to fry myself in the heat of my private hell and write, in spite of refusals and the unawareness, when I couldn't care less and could never have imagined that, one day, I could have loved a woman the way I loved Joana.

AFTER HEARING JOANA'S LAST MESSAGE, I IMAGINED HER WITH ME, HERE IN SÃO PAULO

I am sure that the little whore would love the fat *fogazzas* at Gianotti's. Here, she would notice that my eyes become green when I cry too much, and she would cry with me. At Livraria da Vila, she would discover she had vaginal discharge and some friends in common, and would make sure to catch some jaboticabas from that arrogant tree. She and Bortolotto would hate each other from the very beginning, and of course I would take Bortolotto's side and Joana would be incapable of recognizing my "Thunderbird friendship." After that we would have our first fight, and somehow, after four years, I would officially inaugurate my ivory kitchenette. She would surely find my father's jokes funny and steal an ashtray from the Martins Fontes barbecue restaurant.

In the darkest nights, I would trust Paulinho Sirloin de Tharso and Jacques Brel to be her tour guides. Ten grams of cocaine and a bottle of Arak. The word "rapture" would come to my mind, and I would install a protection net in my terrace, in case enraptured pussycats felt like flying without authorization from the control tower. So, Joana and I would spend our nights without alarm, with nothing to spoil our sadness.

But she never showed up.

In her last message, she said goodbye, telling me that she loved me, and from our first chimpanzee meeting until today, nine months later, when the last message was recorded in my voicemail, she had always stayed with me, day after day. "The difference is that I haven't written a book, my love." She cried a lot, said she felt disgusted with her own body, and that it was the end for her. "Don't forget this, I love you." Somehow, and now definitively, she left me again. And for me, who had written old songs and become another man because of Joana, it was too much.

It was too much for me, and I had asked her not to leave me. I had asked her to dance with me. It was too much because I invented absurd words that only Joana and Jacques Brel could understand, me, who had cried so much, who had hidden, and who had asked her to be the shadow of her shadow, *l'ombre de ta main, l'ombre de ton chien*. It was too much for me, and it served no purpose. Joana left me. I listen to Nina Simone, "My Funny Valentine."

RIO DE JANEIRO, A WEEK AFTER BEING DUMPED

During the week after the chimpanzee night, I rented an apartment in Leme. To be alone, near the ocean. The first time without Joana. The first day she was by my side, the whole time, just as she was the next day...just as she is still and will be tomorrow, after all this time. I had everything I *didn't* want, my own company, a beautiful view of the ocean, Joana and a goddamn book I was to write against my will.

* * *

I cried a lot, much, much more than I could have imagined, for I didn't have the slightest idea that we had, indeed, arrived at the end...I asked Joana, as if she were by my side, to bring back the love that we didn't know how to invent. I wished she would suffer from the absence like I did, and that she would also cry with an ocean view. I don't know, maybe cry because of the melting of the polar caps, because of a curse even, I don't care, or because of any other bullshit. But the fate of the ass-kicking, from that moment on, was really becoming a pool of tears, a raging sea, a sad samba. And I would finally have to accept all the poems and sailing boats, I would be doomed to foretell the shipwrecks of the following days and every day ever after as if they were mine! I condemned myself: for Joana's absence, or her presence, it didn't make any difference,consumed in me until the end.

Well, I could have answered her cry for help, saying that I'd suffered a hard blow and would try to understand the fact that she didn't want to fuck me anymore. Or else, I could have answered saying *no*, I would never be able to have her by my side as a friend, anything but that. One way or another, I didn't need a truce. I wanted to fuck her. So I tried to be sweet and cruel at the same time, making her the only one to blame for the unfortunate circumstances of our meeting. I told her I was in Leme, that I had rented a flat. I sent her an email.

"I cried for you yesterday. If I still have a liver (because my heart is shattered), I'll call you."

I don't really know if I used the word "shattered." What matters is that I wanted her to feel solely responsible (which, at the end of the day, she was) for my liver, heart, bile and all my dramatically shattered organs. I was a fool, I recognize that. It was more or less the same as putting up banners along the walls of the main avenues and announcing my stupid love on billboards. If anyone did something like that to me, I would simply ignore it. Unless Nelson Gonçalves decided to sing "Ébrio" through the loudspeakers, but that would be asking too much.

That was what she did, somehow. She ignored me. Of course, I had embarked out of a suicidal desire, resulting, in the final analysis, in a combination of two people. Alright. But she didn't need to promise me a conservative cut saying, "I spent the whole afternoon shaving just for you." Oh, my God! Joana didn't need to be smeared with lipstick, book the hotel room in advance, and take the pictures she sent me. "Here is where we will fuck the whole night, my love." She didn't need to appeal to supernatural forces, or promise me a life of children and Rio de Janeiro, and she shouldn't have included duvets drying in the autumn sun, and the little Indian, my favourite daughter, going to school protesting, so beautiful, looking like her mom. She shouldn't have included me. Or herself.

I could also have waited to see Joana getting hurt by the post-dumping email I sent her, but I couldn't control myself—of course not. I reached for the telephone and the voice that answered me, at 7 o'clock in the evening, was a sleepy voice of someone who'd pulled an all-nighter, who'd just woken up, telling me "Call me tomorrow. Big kiss."

She must have spent the night sucking cocks in spirals, in that way of hers ("only for you, my love"), the same as she did with me. Naturally, she must have been drunk on whiskey and smeared with lipstick. She had only been fucked in the ass "two or three times before." I remember she made that comment between our second and third time, saying that "being fucked in the ass is like shitting backwards, although that doesn't justify anyone's sexual orientation."

Smart girl. I didn't fall in love with her by chance, "Not even with KY."

One more detail: I didn't put it all inside Joana's ass, and I think what I did was right. I can't forget the chimpanzee night.

However, what I'm calling detachment is what I found, and still find, enchanting about Joana. She has always been the little woman in the story, my "little woman," forever. A sweet girl who calls me in the middle of the night to tell me she has slept with the Frenchman with the red wine name, the housewife I had dreamed of my whole life, who carries the AIDS virus and has the same hips as my mother...and who is even hotter and more pious than Mrs. Rosinha Matheus. Ouch.

It would be perfect if I hadn't spent the whole day crying and looking at the ocean. She had definitely shattered my *pierrot* heart and now I would have to alter my time zone to welcome her to my apartment in Leme, as if she were one of those drag queens (she fucked like a drag queen), or as if I was one of those niggers in Lapa who would fuck her in the ass and shove it all in, two, three, thousands of times. Or worse, I would welcome her as my friend. Joana would visit me as though I could turn my stomach inside out and turn her nights around. As if I, not she, didn't mind killing the following day and would still manage to escape, running after another unnoticed desire. And, there's more—it was as if I, not she, had my whole life ahead of me, waiting on the next corner, unaware. It is worth mentioning, it was as if I was 21, and as if she was all the time I wasted in my forties.

I don't understand. What did she mean by last night's email, "I want to be with you forever, call me"?

I am a fool. That is the only explanation. And she knows it and still trusts me as the obvious idiot I must be. She wants to be by my side "forever." To be honest, I hope Joana didn't suffer a lot last night. I like this girl too much, and I can no longer hold back my tears, or the beautiful view I have of Leme Beach. Everything is so sad, so hard to understand. She wanted to go to the beach with me! Oh, God. What happened?

If I could, I would make an observation. The words "I want to be with you forever" would come with oral sex in spiraling movements and hand-holding, a pussy shaved in a conservative V cut, and mainly, distance from the drag queens who fucked her in the ass. Ah, if I could, I would make a lot of observations and forget her. But that is not possible. And there's more—if I could, I would keep a safe distance from the consummated betrayal and the end that I don't want to accept. But I can't.

The fact is that I love this girl and I know she spends her nights sucking cocks in spirals, taking drugs and being fucked in the ass by drag queens. And I care, and it hurts as if the ass was my own. If I knew the other artifices and charms she uses to pull all-nighters and sleep through the next day, I would love her even more, and would suffer in her place, while she would just have fun and forget me.

Maybe "I want to be with you forever" actually means "I want to be fucked in the ass by drag queens instead of you, because you can't be here". Or "I want to kill you every time you think about me."

I have no doubt that Joana (the paradoxical bitch) loves me as much as a fart from her wet pussy. And here, I make a confession—this is enough for me, and more than I really need. But her soul wouldn't be so precious.

* * *

Joana's share is my share. The subject of Joana matters to me, especially from behind the kiosks along Leme Beach.

Last night, for example, I gave myself some hand jobs and cried over Joana's ass as if it were mine, cried for the abortions and the drinking, all the hangovers and the days after, I cried for all the cocaine sniffed and the antidepressants taken with whiskey, because her life matters to me. Especially from behind the kiosks.

While having a hard-on and going through bouts of crying, I broke the barrier of my glands to pay a tribute to the rapes Joana experienced, the ones suggested and the ones consummated by her father. It was a way to throw her up as she had thrown me up. Then I brought her closer, I called her murders mine, all the holes in Joana's body matter to me. Joana and I are chained to a dead past and to an improbable future. She is the red and I am the black; our marriage is perfect, because only Joana and I could call this abandonment love.

The truth, however, is that my love has no chance of competing against the violent desire of this 21-year-old girl. The least I'd have to do, if she hadn't robbed me of verisimilitude, would be to let desire kill love again. The dirty tool I have at my disposal, therefore, is theoretically nothing more, nothing less than the love I feel for her. Fuck the day after our sex. And there's more—if the desire was killed in that seedy hotel room, all we have left is the love which can never become friendship. I won't accept it, no way!

I wanted to have Joana as my woman, so I didn't wear a condom and for the same reason, I believe, she killed that love with the morning-after pill. Damn it, things happened because of the damn love, not the damn desire! This is my position and I won't give it up.

So I called her and told her that if we weren't going to fuck, she didn't have to come.

"Hi, Joana."

"Hi, darling," (a sleepy, beautiful voice).

"Have you read my email?" (I immediately regretted this stupid question)

"No, I just woke up... I've been sleeping for two days..."

"I'm here, in Leme. I've rented a flat."

"Do you have a camera?"

"Me? No..."

"Let's go to the beach? Or have lunch?" (second yawn)

"Of course, of course."

"Big kiss."

"Joana!"

"Yes?"

"Take note of my address...I'll be waiting."

"Big kiss, my darling." (end of the previous yawn)

Cazzo! She invited me to go to the beach, to have lunch! I just had to pretend I didn't care, which was almost the same thing as not caring at all, although it didn't help me to control my bouts of crying. Coke addict, manipulative bitch, delicious pussy, goddamn telephone that will never ring again. Lunch? Beach? Where? When? Here, in Leme, in my apartment, of course?

She could come just for a fuck. I didn't care. I didn't care if she fooled me again, if she invented a thousand excuses. I wouldn't spend a whole Sunday jerking off in Rio de Janeiro, as a warm-up for a beautiful fuck with the woman I wanted to spend the rest of my life with.

Then I called her again and told her not to come. I said that I hadn't traveled for forty years just to satisfy her little fantasy and then be discarded like trash. Friendship, my ass! I told her that for the first time in my life I wasn't using anyone to write a book, and told her I knew her little intentions to become a writer very well, that we were made of the same stuff, and that I knew my own poison. I told her not to torment me with my own image and form. It would be worse if we spent an enchanted day together, and, after everything, we only had a bad fuck. She told me she wanted my love.

"This is what I have to offer you, Joana."

"I lost your address. Where, in Leme?"

The friendship she proposed to me again was humiliating for both of us. I think I made that very clear. Joana talked to me about lightness. She admitted that she had lost me and that I had nothing to do with that loss! She repeated the phrase "forever and ever" and "don't ask me why" several times. In short, I no longer understood a thing. For the last time, I insisted. I told her that after she'd sent me the picture of her little ass, of her pussy shaved in a conservative cut, of her tits on Valentine's Day, after all the kinky emails and mainly after she brought me back to reality, after we fucked all night like two chimpanzees, after the saddest, most perfect, best story of all times, and after the lie we told together, I told her it was impossible for our affair to change into friendship. Never!

I played dirty. Didn't she want to be a great writer? If it was only for friendship then she'd better not come. She'd better not come for me, if we weren't going to repeat our chimpanzee night, the ice cold beer kisses on the round bed of that seedy hotel. If we weren't going to walk hand-in-hand again around Largo do Machado at five in the morning after we were nearly kicked out from Café Lamas that ancient night one week ago, she'd better not come. I asked her not to fuck with me. I told her to remember our shaky hug before her other thousands of fucks. "Do you remember?"

"Now, get into that taxi and ask me for one last kiss before the car leaves."

...no, no way, a story like this can't end in friendship, my God! I refuse to believe that Joana has only realized her fantasy, fucking her favorite writer, and after everything, love was sacrificed for desire. I don't believe it, I can't admit it, why God?

"What happened, Joana?"

This is why I called her and told her not to come and then I said I'd wait for her, I told her she could come anyway. I loved her. I really embarrassed myself. She cried on her end of the line and I cried on mine, except I cried more, and told her that I was just like her, and that if she didn't come, I'd go back to São Paulo, and that leaving would be better than spending the whole day together trying to be friends. "Friendship, my ass." So she wanted to know if we'd end up as enemies and I told her that wouldn't be enough for us, because I loved her. And for the second time I said, "I love you, come back to me, stay with me," and then I hung up the phone with the hope that Joana would get into the next taxi, and that in 15 minutes we would be fucking like chimpanzees again, despite her shitty fantasies, because we loved each other and that should be enough. What the hell.

Lust. The distance I kept and the love I felt, would that be enough? Would she come? I didn't know. I can only say that I had rented an apartment in Leme, and that I was still waiting for that bitch like a proud male flamingo, playing the seduction game. Joana was the female flamingo. The idea, stupid but funny, pleased me, and soon I was thinking of calendars for the year 2005. March, according to my calculations, would be the month of blue flamingos, the month when the little Indian, my first daughter, my favorite child, would be born, the one who would wear a band-aid to school. If everything happened according to plan, the little girl would throw a tantrum on her first day of school and I would be waiting to rescue her, double parked in front of the building, I would have done anything for that child. But everything went wrong.

Joana called again and told me she loved me. She came up with an excuse, told me some lie, and never showed up.

Travelling by plane

I don't want to cast any doubts about the Capitu I chose. That would be another problem. I shouldn't talk about disappointment. I knew, somehow, she wouldn't come. I know Joana doesn't want me. I know Joana wants me.

I have honestly had enough of this zigzag, this rollercoaster. She betrays me. She loves me. She wants to be by my side "forever and ever." She can't say anything else, tells me not to insist, and has a beautiful scar on her lower stomach. She fucks random women, married women, old men, hobos and beggars. She loves niggers and it's irritatingly banal in this aspect—Copacabana's sewer. A devil, sick with HIV. She fucks hairy men who are no longer fat, romantic men, intellectual men (all three categories fit me), stupid men and innocent souls of all makes, calibers and rivets. Vampire, bloodsucker, clairvoyant, coke addict. Lust without a condom. Crazy, mad bitch, bad actress. Blackmailer. Woman of my life. Pussy.

She doesn't want me. She wants me.

Joana is my uncontrolled cry, my swallowed humiliation, the loss that won't let me go because I still have myself. I have the page that's impossible to turn because I'm the one who's writing the next. So, the right decision to leave and say "fuck everything" is nothing more than the "right decision" and will only increase my burden. It will make me walk through the rain, get drunk and shit my pants, not in vain, but twice as often.

I don't know what to do anymore—let Joana suck cocks for me, smash her face on the wall for me, walk the opposite path, let her live the life I threw away and trade reality for fiction. Or vice-versa. I don't know one thing from another. The flesh should never meet the soul, beauty shouldn't be as sad as solitude and farewells, even though this has been my only wish for forty years, the one story that I should never have told.

That is, after a week in the apartment in Leme, I could stand no more. I started to hear "Samba do Avião" in the opposite way. It was raining in Rio, clouds of Bysmuth Magnesia seemed to strangle the Christ, and in fifty minutes the plane would land in São Paulo. From that moment on, the only thing that remained was Joana's voice recorded on my voicemail, crying for help, "forever, my love." Only that, and "that" was too much for me.

I did not want to understand why I cried so much, but looking down at everything from the airplane window, I allowed myself to lose control, and I cried even more, despite Joana. Actually, I knew exactly what was happening.

Now, it was not only about walking away and leaving it all behind, but about a love that flew with me, a love that hadn't worked out. To leave was to stay, and it couldn't be any different. I really think I deserved the blue flamingos and all those tears...I wasn't actually an ass. I was just suffering for the cloudy day, for the Redeemer Christ strangled by clouds of Bysmuth Magnesia, and for looking down from above at a Guanabara that no longer existed. I cried for Tom Jobim & Vinicius de Moraes, and for forty years and a fifty-minute flight—too little time for Joana and almost an eternity for me, I was leaving.